Brothel

BROTHEL

J. Boyett

SALTIMBANQUE BOOKS

NEW YORK

BY THE SAME AUTHOR

For Pam Carter, Dawn Drinkwater, and Andy Shanks;
they also lived in Conway.

Brothel

1.

They were at the Dixie Café, and Ken was sticking green beans up his nose and leafing through *Hustler* while Joyce talked about her troubles at home. She felt relatively confident that he was still listening. And she got a thrill from the indignation that coalesced around Ken in the family restaurant; he had a talent for getting almost, but not quite, punched in the face. This thing with the porno and the beans in the nose, this was everyday stuff.

"Go ahead and eat," said Ken.

Joyce looked at her meatloaf and country vegetables. "No. I'm sending it back."

"So eat off it and then send it back."

She signaled the waitress, who scowled at the scuzzy photos Ken was poring over. Joyce gave the girl a big conventional smile as she handed her the plate and said, "I'm sorry, this isn't what I ordered." She saw the name tag—HANNAH—and realized that this girl was in her Health class, across town at Central Arkansas University. "I asked for the Light. This is the Regular." Hannah took the plate without a word.

Ken removed a green bean from his nose and popped it into his mouth. Joyce sipped her iced tea. "You're disgusting," she said.

"I'm hot," he countered.

"Almost," she said. "But not quite." Ken was small, but proportioned nicely. His brown hair and goatee were ever so slightly too neat. His big hazel eyes were fine when he wasn't doing weird things with them.

"You know I am," he said. "I'm perfect for a cheerleader like you."

3

"I'm not a cheerleader."

"You look like a cheerleader. You dress like an off-duty one."

"Cheerleaders are blonde. I'm dirty-blonde."

"Are black cheerleaders blonde?"

"Does CAU have any black cheerleaders?"

"Fuck if I know."

"Who's paying for dinner, anyway?"

"Well, I bought the *Hustler*."

"Then you should pay, since you're the one who's going to get us kicked out before we have a chance to eat."

"Fine. Who cares which mom we charge it to. Now, you were saying about your dad?"

"*Step*-dad," she said sweetly, and kicked him in the shin.

"*Ow!*" he cried, loud enough to get attention. As he leaned over to rub the offended area, his right arm shifted down, and his left arm, which held the magazine, shifted up, so that its cover was especially prominently displayed. Joyce rubbed her thighs together and lit a cigarette. The family in the booth across from them abruptly and noisily left, the parents glaring at Joyce and Ken. "Pussies," Ken observed. "Anyway. What were you saying about your *step*-dad?"

"I said he was a dick."

"Because?"

"The usual."

"Which is?"

"You know."

"He felt you up?"

"Well, you couldn't call it that in court."

"What could you call it?"

"I don't know. Being touchy-feely."

"Dude, big hard-ass Marines are not *touchy-feely*. They're red-blooded ass-snatchers."

"Maybe he got in touch with his feminine side."

"It sounds like he got in touch with *your* feminine side."

"Yeah, well. Next Thanksgiving he can keep his baster to himself."

"Aw. Was widdle Joyce wictimized by dat big bad man?"

She raised the back of a hand to her forehead and with the other hand clutched an imaginary string of pearls. Eyes half-closed, she cried: "Oh, *save* me, Kenneth!," sat up straight again and sipped her tea. Who cared that Thanksgiving had been ruined? You could annually count on the whole weekend being ruined anyway, by virtue of the fact that Thanksgiving was in it. And where was that tight-ass bitch with her food? It wasn't like the Dixie Café gave free refills. "Oh, and he called me a whore. See, he does take his steak raw, feminine side or not."

"So hold up. You mean he tried to, you know, get a little some-some, you refused, and he called you a whore? Seems like the opposite. And he meant 'whore' as a *bad* thing?"

"Oh, he didn't say anything at the *time*. Neither *one* of us said anything at the *time*."

"So when did he say it?"

"A few minutes later. At the actual table. In front of everybody. He said I dressed like a whore."

"Were you dressed like one?"

"Yeah. I mean, an expensive one. So?"

"What'd the fam say?"

"Mom laughed like she was all shocked, and went 'Harry!' and then got all prim with me and told me I really *should* have paid more attention to my attire on today of all days."

"So, not just buttloads of support on the Mom front. What about aunts, uncles, cousins? Rugrats?"

"Oh, they're not *my* family. They're not *Mom's* family. They're *his* family."

"Now, Joyce. Y'all're all each other's family now. Here's the story, of a man named Harry. . . . That'd be a good name for a show, wouldn't it? *The Harry Bunch.*"

"*Help! I Married A Troglodyte!*"

"Who married, you or your mom?"

"What's the difference?"

"Damn, stepchild. You want me to kick his jarhead ass?"

"Sure."

5

"All right. I'll have my people call his people, and get them to mail me his ass."

"I wish I *could* get him somehow." As soon as the words left her mouth, Joyce brayed nervous laughter to cover the gaffe, not wanting Ken to hear the real and contemptible need in her voice.

"Why don't you really turn into a whore?" Ken timed his suggestion so that it was made just as Hannah was placing the Light in front of Joyce. The waitress made a noise in her throat and huffed away. "No tip," quipped Ken.

"Why don't I turn into a whore? Why, whatever do you mean, Ken?"

"Just what I said. How pissed off would he be if you were a hooker? That'd piss off any red-blooded American dad."

"*Step*-dad."

"Close enough. Don't kick me again. Anyway, how about it?"

"What if he showed up as a customer?"

Ken made a face and waved his hand like she'd farted. "Don't be nasty."

"All right. I'll think about it."

They turned to their food. Joyce was hungry, and Ken must have been too, since he stopped playing with his food and ate it. The talk drifted toward gossip about Joyce's roommate at the dorm, Mal-short-for-Malinda, and the ditzy suitemate they shared a bathroom with, Sherry. Ken occasionally held up the magazine for Joyce's perusal and demanded a critique of boob or bush or both. After a while he said, "Listen, I'm serious. Why don't you? Become a whore?"

"Oh, sure."

"For real."

"Yeah. I could rifle the Drama department for old *Cabaret* costumes, and go hail pick-ups with Confederate flag bumper stickers down at the end of Burger Row."

"That's, uh, cool, I would videotape that if you had the balls to really do it, but I had in mind something more realistic."

"Fuck off, Ken."

"Joyce. I am really serious. Look at my eyes. I am really, truly serious."

"I can't tell shit from looking at your eyes."

"All right, all right... Hear me out. Just because it's funny doesn't mean I'm joking. Now, you know, and I know, that this town is full of guys who are no more dickheaded than average, who aren't too fat or deformed, and yet are virgins. And both of us furthermore know that most of these guys would give anything—anything!—for one shot at blowing their wad with a real live girl in the room."

"What makes you think I'd want to just fuck a bunch of losers and jerk-offs who couldn't get laid any other way?"

"Joyce. In the eyes, now. That's where I want you looking, because it's honesty time. Joyce, would you or would you not say that every guy you've ever fucked has been a loser jerk-off, anyway?"

She rolled her eyes. "You are such an asshole." This was a different, more intimate version of the thrill she got from watching him push the surrounding diners. She loved proving that she was tough enough to take it when he pushed her.

"The asshole is *always right*. Don't you fools understand?! And would you or would you not furthermore—that's one of my favorite words, 'furthermore'—would you or would you not furthermore say that you have not ever been very selective about *which* loser jerk-off you've fucked? I mean, it's always seemed to me like you just fucked anyone who turned up, anyway. So what's the big deal about getting paid for it? I tell you, when I think about all the pimply, totally amazed retards that you've deflowered for free, I just feel sick."

"Well, I would never fuck *you*."

"Yeah, but that's, like, because we're twin Gods of the Universe, and all of Creation would explode if we copulated."

"Touché."

"Listen. I'm being. Fucking. Serious. A hundred dollars a pop *minimum*. That's *minimum*. A fuck a day could get you three thousand a month. That's, like, thirty-six thousand dollars a year, man."

"That's also screwing some geek every day!" She refused to speak more softly than Ken, and took fluttering pride in the heads that turned at *her* remarks.

"All right. Fine. One asshole a week. You do that now. That would still be four hundred a month, which is more than you'd make at *Waffle* House. Where you've been *talking* about working. And this is money for doing something you already do for *free*. I mean, Jesus, Joyce."

Now she felt confused. It was hard to remember why the whole thing had been inconceivable thirty seconds ago. "But...." The Light meatloaf congealed in its own grease on her plate. "But it's *illegal*, right? I mean, even *beer's* illegal in Conway."

"Beer's not illegal. It's only illegal to sell it."

"Yeah, well, same thing."

"Oh, hey, that's right!... Anyway, who *cares*? And who'll find out?"

"As if people at CAU wouldn't talk about a hooker on campus."

"Not on campus. My apartment is a five-minute walk away."

"Okay, you just hold that weird thought. Now, seriously. People would talk, and I'd wind up in jail for prostitution."

"No you wouldn't."

"Oh? Why not?"

"Because ... okay, listen. People will talk, sure, but that'll be no big deal. We can cut the talk by, well, twenty percent, maybe, if we tell our clients they'll be blacklisted if we ever catch them blabbing. Even so, word'll spread like wildfire. Like *wildfire*. I'll have to beat people off with a stick to keep you down to only one fuck a day."

"You're so poetic."

"Don't worry about the *law*, though. What're people going to say when they call the cops to complain? 'Officer, there's a fucking bordello on Baridon Street'? The cops'll laugh it off. At worst, we'll have to give them a discount. And if it comes to that, we'll take it out of my cut."

"What if they do come and try to bust us?"

"What will they find then? I'll be in the living room watching *The Simpsons*. You'll be in the back doing some guy. What could be more natural in a sleepy churchy little college town? I mean, I won't be wearing a pimp hat with a big green ostrich feather in the headband. There won't be a red light over the screen door. 'What, Officer? Someone called in a brothel? That's the darnedest. . . . Why, no, sir, that just bewilders the daisies out of me. . . . Well, yes, sir, I guess I do have a few enemies, a few thousand, that is. . . . Oh, you know, sir, the usual, just a lot of ex-girlfriends and their ex-boyfriends, ha ha ha. . . . These two, sir? Oh, this is just a buddy of mine and his date. . . . Well, sir, no, they're not married, as a matter of fact. . . . I know, I know, but what can one Christian do? . . . All right. Well, see you, Officer, and thanks for your concern!'"

There was a long silence between them then. Neither moved. Ken leaned forward, kid-stuff *Hustler* forgotten, elbows on the table, hands stretched toward her in the closest thing she'd ever seen on him to supplication. She folded her arms over her chest, chewing the inside of her cheek. "Understand: me talking about this hypothetically is not me agreeing. Cool?"

"Cool, cool."

"I would never—even if this weren't totally nuts—I would never do this alone. If I'm going to be, like, a total outcast from decent female society, I would need at least one person to be out there with me. At least one."

"Okay. I got to say, I think more than two would be a security risk, but okay, two's cool."

He was being weird; he was never this pliable. Joyce realized that he had never before wanted so badly for her to do something. He was totally serious about this brothel thing. She felt herself teetering closer than ever before to that edge, and dared herself to look over the rail. "And if the cops come by once, that's it. Party's over. I buy your spiel about being able to get out of it once, with smooth talking. But twice? In a town like this? No fucking way."

9

"All right, I think you're pussying out there, but I can deal with it."

"And another thing. What's all this about the brothel being at your apartment and you being my pimp?"

"Yeah, yours and whoever else's. What about it?"

"Bitch, I don't need a pimp, bitch, is what's about it."

"Oh. Oh, Jesus. Oh, okay, I see." Ken thrust himself back in his seat with feigned indignation. "So where do *you* want to put the brothel? At your dad's house? Step-dad's, I mean."

"What's wrong with my dorm room?"

"Um, nothing, unless being the stupidest idea of all time counts. The least thing wrong with it is that Mal would probably have to be in on it. That's probably fine. But everything else. . . . I mean, you're nervous about the pigs being nosey, but you don't think the RAs in the girls' wing of Short-Denny Hall are going to be a problem? They're like the nosiest, most self-righteous people of all time. As soon as they smell a whiff of whorehouse they're going to be pounding on your door and telling you to pack your bags. They'll harass every guy you sign in. I mean, the cops have to follow the law, at least in theory. But the RAs only have to follow *dorm regulations*."

"Okay, okay. Dorm's a dud. But what's so great about your place? And what makes you think you could be my pimp?"

"My place is easy to find. It's got two bedrooms, a living room and a kitchen, all of which you can fuck in—believe me, I know—and I'd be an awesome pimp."

Joyce's arms came uncrossed and she picked at her food. "Well, why would I need you for a pimp? You don't think I could get guys on my own?"

Ken held his face utterly blank and earnest. "You'd really feel comfortable walking up to guys and saying, 'Hey, I'll bang you for a hundred bucks?' I mean, I'd feel awesome saying it *for* you. But how would *you* really feel?"

"I'd probably only have to do it once or twice, then word of mouth would get around."

"Whatever. Anyway, you're forgetting that you'll need me for the same reason hookers always need pimps, for protection."

"Protection? What's he going to do, rape me? He already knows I'm going to fuck him." She reminded herself that they were only joking.

Ken threw up his hands. "Jesus, don't you ever watch those cop movies with those whore-killers in them? What if he gets kicks out of beating up girls? What if he's like a religious fanatic and brings a snake with him? What if he's a twenty-four-incher who's going to rip you in half? What if he's determined to scoop your poop, or money-shot in your face? Gross! Barf out! What if he gets belligerent and refuses to wear a condom? That's where I come in. I'll be sitting in the next room the whole time. All you've got to do is let out a yell, and I'll come running in and wallop him with my spiked bat."

"Your *what?*"

"My spiked bat."

"Your *what?* Your *what* did you say? Your spiked *what?*"

"My spiked bat."

"What is that?"

"Duh. It's like a bat, except with a big old rusty nail sticking out of it."

"Do you have one of those?"

"Naw, Joyce. I'm going to make it. I always wanted one, I just never had an excuse before."

They fell silent for a while. Ken played with his green beans and Joyce scrutinized her plate.

"Well?" demanded Ken.

"I'm thinking."

"You're going to ask Mal, aren't you? That'd make the most sense. Anyway, if you were actually considering doing it in y'all's dorm room, you must be planning to invite her."

"I wasn't 'actually considering' *anything*, Ken, because we were just fooling around."

"Bullshit. You're in."

"Not necessarily. Anyway, we haven't talked about your cut. I won't put up with a bunch of exorbitant nonsense."

"I'll be ecstatic with a very low cut. But you're so in."

"Fuck off. You don't know me."

"Again, bullshit. I triple-dare you."

"Ken. . . ."

"I triple-*dog*-dare you."

"Ah, shut up."

They weren't making any effort not to be heard by the nearby booths. A stern bald dry-faced man of late middle age, a real pillar of the community, some kind of farmer-cum-deacon, appeared at Joyce's shoulder and glowered at her: "Now listen here. If you're going to come and eat around decent people I wish you'd shut your filthy—"

"Fuck off, sour grapes," she said, and flicked her hand scornfully at him. Ken burst into jeering, exaggerated laughter, pointing his right index finger at the man. "Busted!" he cried. The old guy could not hit a girl. He might have hit Ken, had Ken not been gripping a steak knife, pointed up, in his left hand. The man stalked off. Ken leaned across the table to slap Joyce a high five. "You are so in."

"Not yet I'm not."

"You're so in and you don't even know it."

"I don't know. Probably not. God, this is crazy."

Now a blushing manager appeared, also trying—albeit less successfully—to be stern. He explained that there had been several complaints and that he was sorry to have to ask them to leave. Joyce and Ken commiserated, meanwhile shoveling food into their mouths as the increasingly flustered manager kept explaining that, no, they really did have to leave right away. Once their plates were clean they got up and the manager followed them to the register, where Joyce had trouble counting out the money. The trained and stabilized part of herself blithely knew that this couldn't happen, but from her soul's crow's nest she saw better; she'd already dared herself.

2.

When Joyce entered the dorm room black-haired Mal was perched in the windowsill smoking a cigarette, gazing out at the new-laid dark. Their windows faced the boys' wing across the barren courtyard, but Mal was looking toward the street. "Ken drop you off?" she asked. She was damp and scrubbed, fresh from the shower; she wore a white T-shirt so stretched-out and shapeless as to be modest, even though she had on nothing else but panties.

Joyce lit a cigarette. She looked at the *Cat People* poster Mal had hung up—Mal got a kick out of old film noir movies. "I'm an attractive woman. I might've been out on a real date."

"Were you?"

"No. I was with Ken."

"You're predictable."

"Well, I did Geoff in the bathroom at Vino's last week after his gig. Was *that* predictable?"

"From you?"

"Fuck off."

"You're predictable when you're around Ken."

"It only looks that way because he's so totally unpredictable, and so I fade in comparison."

"No he isn't."

"You want to hear something unpredictable we came up with tonight?"

"Shoot." Mal lit a new cigarette off the old one.

Joyce took a drag to stall for time. Her belly was buzzing. There was no telling which way Mal would go, and when Joyce announced the idea she had to be ready to either laugh

13

it off, or else lay serious plans. She eyed a big black scar in the plastic mattress from where she had once fallen asleep with a lit cigarette. "Well, we were thinking about setting up a brothel."

Mal looked at her. "Do what?"

"A brothel. A cathouse. I suggested setting it up right here in the dorm, but Ken talked me out of that, it'd be too indiscreet. So then we decided on his apartment. It's right near campus and all, it's real convenient." She kept a hint of a smile on her face and watched Mal closely for the cue as to what kind of smile it should end up being.

Mal gazed into space, lifting the cigarette to her mouth again. "So is Ken the protection, or is he getting someone else?"

Shit. They really were going to do this. "It's just him," Joyce said.

"Do you trust him?"

"More or less."

"He's kind of a little guy."

"Yeah, but he says he's going to have a spiked bat."

"A what?"

"A spiked bat. He says that's a bat with a rusty nail sticking out of it."

"Well … okay. That's a pretty good deterrent. But if he ever actually hits anyone with it, show's over."

"Yeah. That's, uh, that's kind of what I said. To Ken." She wanted to scream at Mal: *Are you nuts?! I grew up going to Methodist Youth Group and you grew up going to a Baptist one! Our parents pay for everything! We're in Conway!* But at the same time she was thrilled. Terrified, too. "Like, of course the whole spiked bat thing would be kept in reserve. For emergencies. You could kill someone with a thing like that. Especially if it's actually rusted."

Mal shrugged and ashed her cigarette. "So Ken's the pimp, huh. What about the girls?"

"Well, we want to keep the numbers low. As in, two would be plenty."

"Sounds reasonable."

"But also, two's minimum. If I'm one of them, that is. I would just feel really uncomfortable doing it alone." She laughed. "I guess that's pretty silly, huh?"

Mal didn't answer. "If you're one girl, then who's the other?"

"As a matter of fact, Mal, I was going to ask you."

"Okay. How much are y'all talking about charging?"

"We hadn't discussed it just a whole lot. I think the last number we said was a hundred dollars."

"A hundred-fifty."

"Jeez. That seems pretty expensive."

"A hundred-fifty. Trust me. They can afford it. They'll pay anything, and there's nowhere else for them to go in this white-flight suburb. And what do they know about cheap or expensive when it comes to pussy? What do you know about it, for that matter? Or me? What other prices are there to compare it to? I could go on the internet and look up the going rate for a prostitute in Mexico City, or in the Netherlands, or at the Mustang Ranch. But there's nobody in the world who can tell me the going rate in Conway, Arkansas because it hasn't gone yet. Not out in public. A hundred-fifty."

"All right . . . shit, that's pretty good money. Like, just four times a month and you'd get six hundred dollars."

"Tax-free, too. If we work a little harder, we can buy ourselves cars. Is Ken going to be a problem about money?"

"What do you mean?"

"I mean, is Ken going to be a problem about money? Is he going to all of a sudden insist on, like, a twenty percent cut or something?"

"I don't know. I don't think he's in it for the money."

"Of course he isn't. He's already rich. He's in it for the same reason he's in anything, to stir up shit. But we might get a couple weeks into it and then him decide a fun way to stir up shit would be to demand half the money or something stupid."

"Well, I would never vouch for Ken, exactly. But I think he'd only do something like that if he was really bored, and

15

I figure it'll take even him a pretty long time to get bored with being a pimp."

"Fair enough. But y'all didn't actually talk about numbers?"

"He said he would be ecstatically happy with even a tiny cut."

"Then I won't agree to more than five percent. And I'll try to talk him down from that. Not that his job isn't worth more. If we were coming up with this shit on our own and hiring some guy I'd offer him a lot. But not Ken, he's already going to be having too much fun. I bet he'd do it for free."

"Okay. I'll let you handle the, like, negotiations."

"All right." Mal blew out a cloud of smoke. "Anything else?"

"Um. Well, no. I can't think of anything. There is the whole recruitment thing. But Ken's handling that, too."

"Fine. We still have plenty of time to hash that sort of stuff out."

"All right. . . . I guess that's it, then!" Joyce lay stretched-out on the bed and laughed delightedly. "Holy shit, Mal. Holy shit."

Mal grinned over at her. "We're going to make a lot of money."

"Jesus, we're going to do a lot more than that."

"We sure are."

"Oh my God. Oh my God! Oh my God."

"Be cool, kiddo."

"I am so totally fucking cool. Dude, I am bad-ass."

"That's right."

They looked at each other and grinned like little girls at a slumber party, clutching pillows to their flat chests and planning elaborate future weddings. . . . Then came a gentle rapping on the door to the bathroom, which connected their room to Sherry's.

3.

"You did *what?*" said Ken.

"We told her she was in." They were at Wendy's, sitting at a red plastic-mold table beside a scuffed Plexiglass window. This was the Wendy's at the end of Burger Row, not the one by Wal-Mart. Although Burger Row's source was in the middle of Conway's downtown, here, a mere mile or so later, they were already nearly at its mouth, at one of the last fast-food joints before the blue road spluttered into a brief surf of white shining car dealerships and then opened into an expanse of half-inhabited green and brown, the town gone. "We told her it was cool."

"Whoa, hold up. Not only did you tell her—*Sherry*—tell Sherry she was in, but you told her it was *cool?* Hang on now. I beg to differ."

"Ken, this is not a big deal."

"Cosmically speaking, it's not. Sucks for us, though."

"It's fine. Look, she's pretty. She fucks. She'll do."

"Maybe we should name the place Dumb Bitches R Us."

"Hey now. Don't you forget who two-thirds of those bitches are. And especially one third."

"Yeah, you and Mal. Y'all're the dumb bitches who told Sherry she could join."

"Will you stop being a whiny little bitch? You said two was fine, security-wise. So I got two, Sherry and Mal."

"Oh, man. Did you just say that? Two! Two! You and Mal! Not you, Mal, and Sherry, which, if you'll notice, is three."

"Oh."

"Uh-huh. Man. That's it, the name is now definitely Dumb

17

Bitches R Us. Don't worry, I'll count myself as one of the bitches."

What had happened the night before was this: Sherry had opened the door and entered while still knocking, pretending to tip-toe with her back bent and her shoulders hunched up, laughing and waving her hand in front of her face and saying, "Gee, it sure is *smoky* in here!"

She bummed a cigarette from Mal, explaining that she'd taken up smoking as an appetite suppressant. ("Couldn't hurt," shrugged Mal.) "Because," Sherry continued, "we've got to stay *attractive*." She leaned forward at the waist and swung her upper body from side to side, first towards Mal and then towards Joyce, one hand on her hip, the other raised and level with her head, the cigarette still burning between her fingers. "Don't we, girls? *All* of us do."

"What do you mean, Sherry?" calm, cool Malinda calmly coolly asked.

"What do you mean, Sherry?" calm, cool Malinda calmly coolly asked, thought Joyce.

Sherry rolled her eyes. "Uh. I totally heard you guys. I was using the *toilet*. The one we *share*. If y'all were going to be all Norad about it, you should've made sure no one was on the pot."

They wrangled with Sherry over whether they'd allow her in. "It's just a matter of numbers," Joyce lied. "If we have too many people, it won't be safe."

"*Hello!*" said Sherry, and flung out her hands. She had forgotten she was holding her cigarette—it went spinning to the floor with a spray of orange sparks, and Sherry cut herself off as she scrambled to retrieve it. Once upright, she sternly pointed the cigarette at Joyce, like a schoolmistress with a pointer. "*Hello!* Haven't you ever heard of safety in numbers! I don't remember ever hearing of safety in—you know—absences!"

They couldn't just say, "It's not that you're unsexy"—her blonde hair was better-kept than Joyce's, her blue eyes matched her sweater, her cheekbones were enviable—"it's just that you're kind of a stupid annoying big-mouthed faker and we don't want to play with you." Besides, Sherry had flipped her hair and grimly pronounced, "Anyway. If I'm not *in*, then I'm *telling*. So *there*." And, as Mal had said, "Well, if otherwise you're going to tell, you're in."

Now, at the Wendy's, Ken cussed glumly.

Joyce looked through the window and across the four-lane street at a car dealership, all festive chrome and flags. She picked at her small dry spud, reminiscing about when they used to have a self-serve potato bar, and you could scoop on gallons of oily cheese sauce and pounds of bacon bits. She'd been a kid then, and unworried about her ass. Nowadays your meager portion was doled out behind the counter, and they'd hardly given her enough cheese sauce to moisten the potato enough for it to be gag-downable. "Quit messing around," she said. "If you bum me out, I'll drop the whole idea. And then you'll be alone with Sherry."

"And Mal."

"Yeah, but she won't laugh at your dumb jokes."

"She'd fuck me, though."

Joyce nearly spat out the Mr. Pibb she was sucking up the straw. Ken grinned. Would Mal ever be down for that? Despite everything, there was something similar about those two. Ken had never expressed any such intentions towards Mal, but, as Joyce had insisted, he was unpredictable. Take that time they'd snuck into the Honors lounge to sit on the nice couches and watch the big-screen TV. No one was supposed to be up there except Honors students and their escorted guests, but fuck it; there had been no one else around, and she and Ken had watched *Seinfeld*. They started fucking with each other, and pretty soon he was grabbing her tits and squeezing them while she tried to swat his hands away. Joyce had never been aware before of any sort of chemistry or sexual tension between them, nor was she aware of any chemistry, exactly, now. Ken was just grabbing her tits, laughing and making a game out of it. Joyce told him to quit it, and slapped at him, but she had to giggle and laugh because if she revealed that she was really serious, she'd be a spoilsport. She refused to crack before Ken did. But Ken would never crack. And so he got to spend twenty minutes groping her big tits because he refused to acknowledge that they were serious. Brilliant! She was determined to learn everything.

Over the next couple days Ken prepared the brothel. There wasn't much for Joyce to do. Mal and Sherry asked her, with some trepidation from Sherry, about how the johns were being recruited. She took their queries to Ken, who laughed and gave her a theatrical wink. "*Oh,* yeah. Y'all don't worry about *that.*"

Joyce smiled icily. "No bullshit, Ken."

"Oh, no, no, no."

"No sick shit, Ken." She had a sudden vision of the three scantily-clad girls strutting in to find their respective fathers—step-father, in her case—reclining on beds of Turkish pillows, or bean bags: trembling, nude, and unsuspecting. But she could not mention this scenario, lest she inspire Ken. "I'm for real. You go all unpalatable on me, and I'll walk."

"You never have before."

"This is different. This is genitals."

"Dude, don't worry. I am so smooth, and I associate only with other smooth people. Like you, for instance. Forget about Sherry for now. Anyway, it stands to reason that the customers I procure will also be smooth."

"Shut up and listen for a second. Bear in mind that our ideal boy is one who hasn't ever gotten laid, and who doesn't think he ever can get laid. Not guys who *really* can't ever get laid. No psychos. No really fat guys with runny noses. And I'm sorry, I feel like a bitch for saying this: but no harelips. Also no hunchbacks."

"You prejudiced piece of shit. You white-bread, cheerleading piece of Estée Lauder shit."

"Clairol, motherfucker."

"Clearasil, maybe."

"Fuck off, apeface. Look. *Skinny* guys. Guys in glasses who never make passes. Cowlicks: acceptable. Acne scars indicating a confidence-crippling zit-clogged past? Good. Actual confidence-crippling acne in the here and now? Bad."

"Hey, don't worry, I'm on it."

"When you pick out a john, just remember to ask yourself one key question: 'Would I fuck this guy?'"

"Done. You'll find a bunch of really fey skinny dudes with limp wrists and scarves, all of them wondering what the hell they're supposed to be doing with you."

"Don't screw this up. It'll be a lot funnier if we actually go through with it than if we all just barf and go home."

"All right. But I can slip in a *couple* of interesting ones, yeah?"

"Jesus! *No one interesting!*"

The day before they opened for business, Ken invited all three girls to his place and gave them the tour in a wide-eyed mock-grandiloquent manner. Joyce was amused—Ken rarely failed to amuse her—and she followed Ken through his half of the duplex with a smirk. Mal was expressionless. Sherry took her cue from Joyce and just kept grinning, whether Ken was making a joke or not.

First he took them to his bedroom. "I'm basically leaving everything like it is. Except I'll change the sheets after y'all fuck on them. Whoever fucks in this room will owe me a six-percent cut. That's, like, nine dollars, I guess."

He took them to the back bedroom. Because it faced the backyard, this had been his pot sanctuary. Now there was a stained Salvation Army twin mattress in the middle of the room. It wasn't even lined up straight with the walls. "I was just going to leave it like that," he explained, "not even put sheets on it or anything. Whoever works in here owes me two percent."

"Put sheets on it," commanded Joyce. "And change them between every rut."

"Okay, fine. Three percent. An even four-fifty. The math's easier, anyway."

"What's with all the shoes and shirts and shit on the floor?" asked Mal, once they were back in his bedroom.

Ken opened the door to his walk-in closet. Most of its contents had been kicked or thrown out into the bedroom, although a few shirts and pants still dangled on their hangers. Squeezed into the closet, lying on the floor, was another thrift store mattress, this one more ancient than the last. Its urine stains formed the map of an alien world. "This is the third office," he said. "It's a little tight, so you'll probably have to bend your knees to close the door. I got the shortest mattress they had. Whoever does it in here owes me one percent. That's a dollar-fifty."

"Dibs on the closet, then," said Mal. "You're going to get sheets for this mattress, too, and it's still only going to be a dollar-fifty cut."

"Sheesh, all right. Why not? I'm made of money."

"Well, Ken, this is all very. . . ." Joyce paused, searching for the precisely wrong word. "Elaborate."

Ken feigned hurt. "But what about the sign?" On the front door he had taped a piece of white posterboard, upon which he had crudely executed the word BROTHEL in a boisterous three-dimensional bubble font, with blue, purple, orange, and brown markers.

Sherry didn't realize they were joking. "It's all *right*," she said magnanimously, putting one hand on her hip and cocking it. Ken rolled his eyes at Joyce as he led them back to the living room.

"Oh!" said Joyce. "I almost forgot to ask about the spiked bat!"

Ken snapped his fingers. "Crap! And that's the main event, too!"

"Is it ready?"

"Naw, but don't worry, it will be by showtime. But y'all hold up, don't leave yet. I'll read you the speech I'm going to give all the customers about it."

"Speech?"

"Yeah, you know, some dazzling garbage to scare the bejesus out of them from the get-go, so they don't get any ideas." He rushed off, leaving the three of them in the living room.

None of them had anything to say to the other two, but Sherry shrugged off that inconvenience. "Y'all, isn't this *wild*! I swear, this is exactly the kind of crap my family is always getting into. Like, I really hope we don't end up like my cousin did in Orlando. Her name's Gabby. I know, what a stupid name! Anyway, her name's Gabby, and, like, she was a hooker too, in Orlando, except, you know, not in as safe a way as us. Like, she did it really dumb. Anyway, what *happened* was—this is after all that hooker stuff, though, this is when she stole a car—I mean, *she* didn't steal it, I *believe* her, but she was mixed up with all these weird scuzzy dudes and—anyway, what *happened* was—"

Ken hurried back into the room. In his hand was a piece of notebook paper so crumpled, creased, and limp that it looked like it had been balled up in the pocket of some jeans that had been tossed into a washing machine. "Okay, y'all, here's the caveat all the customers are going to get."

Sherry smiled tightly. "Ken," she said. "*Excuse* me. I was *talking*."

"I know, hold on, I was up all night writing this." Ken held the paper up in front of his face, cleared his throat, and began to declaim in a monotone, eyebrows drawn together as he did his impression of someone who'd only just learned to read. "Gentleman, you now see here in my hand a spiked bat." He held up his empty hand, posing like the Statue of Liberty. Glancing at them he dropped out of oratorical mode to say, "Pretend I got it already." Then he continued: "In elementary school I was a star Little Leaguer, and in those days of yore I was oft known to knock the ball out of its cover, just like Robert Redford in that movie *The Natural*. Believe me, my friend, that gift has not been lost. If you are a good man, of true heart, like Launcelot in that movie *Excalibur*, then you need not fear me. But if ye be a Mordred, beware my lusty smiting. If you are good, I will merely sit on this sofa and eat my cheesy poofs, avec docility. But should mine ears detect even a whimper of fear or horror from this nice young lady, I will burst into the appropriate room like the wrath of God and wallop thee with this here spiked bat." Once more he raised the imaginary bat. "Sir, I am but a small man. But lapse not into foolishness, for the spiked bat is a large man, and his throbbing instrument of both love and murder will seek out thy softest parts, to be sure. To be sure, should you incur its wrath, never or rarely again will you suffer injuries more painful, or more embarrassing to explain to the police, or to your bodacious mom when you ask her for her credit card so you can pay off the doctor. That having been said, sir, I hope that you shall sample our delicious wares with both honor and restraint, and cum and go in peace, so that we may remain friends and continue in this supercalifragilisticexpialidocious arrangement, or relationship." Lowering both the paper and the imaginary spiked bat, he looked at Joyce. "Should I say 'thine' instead of 'thy'?"

"I think 'thy' is fine. I don't think it matters." She raised an eyebrow. "You spent all night writing that?"

He nodded. "It was mainly a process of revision."

4.

On opening night Joyce took some extra time to make herself up and so was running late. She spent twenty minutes choosing which of her three perfumes she should use, and painstakingly applied some eyeliner her grandmother had given her for her birthday. Holy shit, what had she done? On a whim she'd become a whore! A real one, not just an easy lay in the backseat, but a slag who accepts cash in return for sex with total strangers. Fuck it, though. While she had technically "known" pretty much all the guys she had ever fucked, had that made any difference?

She briefly hoped that Ken had recruited guys so hideous and nasty that there would be no protests when the girls simply walked out. Immediately she felt ashamed of her weakness, and was on the verge of flouncing defiantly out of the dorm when her blood turned to cold mucous and she realized she had not yet really made herself presentable: not shaved her bikini line, etc. What if she hadn't remembered until she was doing the deed, exposed to some bumpkin's cruel laughter? She made herself even later, what with stripping off her clothes and shaving in the shower. Plus she had to brush her teeth. She leaned into the bathroom mirror and plucked stray eyebrow hairs till she cried. And there was a small cyst on her leg which she attempted to pop, but she only managed to inflame it. She almost forgot to reapply the perfume before leaving—she'd tried hard not to get her eyeliner wet in the shower.

When she finally got to Ken's his front door, still bearing its BROTHEL sign, was propped open. "Glad you could join us," he said, his voice oozing mock-scorn. "It's only the premiere.

Won't you come in?"

"I thought I'd be fashionably late."

Three dudes sat cross-legged on the stained carpet. Joyce smiled at them, with a hint of a leer. They weren't ugly enough for her to get out of anything. Besides, Mal and Sherry were already snuggled up under their assignments' arms, hands resting on the guys' denimed knees. Sherry nevertheless looked at Joyce with an expression that made it clear she expected to be rescued if the need arose. Mal seemed distantly amused. At least Joyce had been spared the necessity of choosing which guy she would go with. The odd man out looked sheepishly at her, a chubby boy with a red, slightly pock-marked face.

"All right," said Ken, "now that Princess has finally arrived, maybe we can get on with things. I guess introductions are in order. So, Joyce, Mal's mark is Phil, Sherry's is Joe, and this lonely dude is Gregory. Y'all, this is Joyce."

"Oh, yeah, we, uh . . . I know who *Joyce* is," stammered Gregory.

Joyce studied him. If they had met, he'd failed to make an impression on her. Then again, he was a forgettable type. Suddenly she realized that none of the guys she had ever slept with had seemed as sweet as this virginal little whoresniffer, and she sank down to the carpet and curled up beside him, as Ken dashed out of the room. Joyce continued to smile coquettishly at Gregory—she was afraid that if she changed her expression she wouldn't be able to get it back—and tried not to be alarmed by Ken's sudden exit. Mal and Sherry didn't seem concerned. Their boys didn't look any better than Joyce's, physically, and they didn't have his sweet aura. Gregory had turned even redder and was staring at Joyce with open wonder. This whole prostitution gig wasn't bad. Nobody seemed able to think of anything to say, though.

Joyce noticed that everyone else had a big blue plastic cup of red wine just as Ken reappeared with a cup for her. She took a big swallow. It was probably from a box. Ken sat on the floor before them, in the spot that in a normal living room would have been occupied by a television. In its buried roots his expression was probably a smile. He said cheerfully to Joyce, "Mal was just telling us that she died in high school."

Joyce blinked and turned to Mal.

"Only for a minute," Mal explained.

"A *whole* minute?" said Sherry. "Because, you know, I heard that can cause *brain* damage."

"It may not have been that long. I wasn't conscious, you know, seeing as how I was dead. Later, the other kids told me it had been about a minute, but they weren't sure."

"Oh, I don't mean it's *impossible*. Brain damage might start after one minute, but an awful lot of people stay dead longer than that. Like, two minutes, or five minutes, or maybe even ten minutes. They just get more brain-damaged, is all."

"Mal?" Joyce said. "What the fuck're you talking about?"

"I sort of died once in high school. My heart stopped along with my breathing, for just a minute. More or less. Everybody else's already heard the story. It'd be rude for me to repeat it."

"Aw, but little old *me* didn't hear it," Joyce said. "These boys won't mind if you tell *me* what happened." She batted her eyes vigorously at the johns, which was meant to be a grotesque parody of the situation. But then she realized that, in these circumstances, the gesture passed. Her Betty-Boop-on-crack fit the moment perfectly, and no one batted an eye but her.

Mal glanced over the three guys, then locked eyes with Joyce and began her tale. "It was some lame canoe trip in the tenth grade. My church youth group. One weekend we went to float the river. Out near the Ozarks, you know. Way out in the woods. There was one pool where the water was cold and where most of us beached our canoes—these rented plastic canoes— and went swimming in our clothes. At first I thought the water was dirty, because it was brown. Then I realized the rocks at the bottom were brown and the water was perfectly clear. In one corner I found a half-decomposed white salamander, maybe a foot long. He was on his back in a shallow part of the pool."

"Okay," said Joyce. "So the salamander tried to kill you...?"

"Fine, I'll get to the point. We all swam in our clothes. The chaperones got pissed because they said being wet would reveal our body-shapes indecently. They were Baptists. We were all Baptists. I was surprised, since I'd figured that being totally dressed made it impossible to be revealing. Besides, I was wearing like a fucking cast-iron bra.

"So there was this boy in the youth group, Robby. He was a real horn-dog around me. Sometimes he was sweet; like, the Sunday School class always had doughnuts and orange juice, and he would always get me some. You know, 'Hey, Malinda, can I carry your Bible?,' that kind of thing. Lots of times, he touched me. On the arm. On the back. On the lower back. On the lower lower back. I'd tell him to fuck off—except I never did exactly, because we were usually at church, and back then I never would have said 'fuck,' period. Instead I mostly ignored him, except once in a while I'd whine and say 'Hey' or something lame and shrug him off. Even that was enough to mortify him. Never enough so he'd quit for real, though. He was kind of a scuzzbag."

"Now, now," Ken warned, "that's not very good whore-talk."

"Oh, yeah. Sorry, guys. Anyway, Robby appointed himself my canoe partner, and I was too much of a pussy to fight about it, especially in front of all those other kids, who thought Robby was really sweet and shy and that I'd be lucky to get a boy like him. He was one of our own. We'd all been in the same youth group together since we were four. So he sat behind me in the canoe. There were more than ten canoes altogether, but we were pretty spaced out, and the river curves around a lot, so there were plenty of times when a single canoe could be isolated. Way to go, chaperones. Anyway, whenever we were out of sight, Robby would get all touchy-feely. I'd hear him put his oar down in the canoe and then I'd hold my breath until I felt his fingers on my neck and shoulders. He'd say he was going to give me a massage because I'd been working so hard. His fingers were like spiders—*you* know. And he wouldn't just massage my shoulders, he'd massage my whole back. And he had a pretty broad definition of 'back.' It went all the way around to my sides, high up under my armpits. Basically all the way around to my tits. And he was nice and solicitous of my lower back as well. He was such a sweetie that he'd stop at nothing to relieve my lower back stress, including sticking his fingers down the waistbands of my pants and panties. Most of the time I'd suffer quietly and try to keep rowing. Or I'd whine and wiggle and he'd quit for a second. Finally, when he tried to stick his hand down the back of my pants for the fourth or fifth time, I turned around and screamed at him to keep his nasty fingers out of my butt and called him a sicko pervert. I really screamed, too. I felt crazy."

Ken was listening with uncharacteristic attention. Sherry sighed. "Jeez, it's hard to imagine you losing your cool and yelling at *anybody*."

"It was the last time I ever really did."

"Because he killed you, right?" said Joyce.

"He did kill me. Everyone on the river must have heard me scream—sound carries over water. He turned blood red. Meanwhile, I'd dropped my oar in the water. It was like my hands had just snapped open while I was screaming at Robby, without me noticing, and the oar had fallen out. It was already floating off, so I half-stood up and leaned out of the canoe to reach for it. And Robby rocked the canoe, as hard as he could without tipping it—just an impulsive bit of spite. I tumbled out. You know how dinky and shallow these rivers get sometimes. Most of this one wasn't very wide. When he tipped me out, we were near the bank and there were a bunch of rocks just under the water, and I smashed my head on one and it knocked me out. So there I was, unconscious, floating face-down. Drowning, basically."

"You mean that asshole didn't even drag you out of the fucking *water*?" demanded Phil. Although outrage would have been a sound amorous strategy, his seemed authentic enough.

"He freaked out. It wasn't that he was all cold-blooded, and definitely not that he'd meant for me to drown. And the only thing that kept him from screaming even louder than I did was that he was crying too hard. He did try to turn the canoe around, all by himself with the one oar, so he could go back and find one of the chaperones and get help. He figured he had a better chance of meeting one coming the other way than of catching up with one of the ones ahead of us."

Joyce laughed. "In this big-ass emergency he tried to paddle back upstream?"

"Yup."

"Why didn't he just jump out and drag you to land?"

"It's the type of guy Robby was. Anything he could do, he figured someone else could do better. And he assumed that something as important as rescuing a drowning girl was too big to be trusted to a guy like him. Which turned out to be a self-fulfilling prophecy."

"What a dick."

"Well. Anyway, one of the chaperones came floating around the bend. This cool youngish guy, named Kent. When it wasn't the Lord's day he worked as a paramedic. He saw me floating face-down and jumped in and swam after me. Dragged me ashore, gave me mouth-to-mouth and CPR. When I woke up, he told me that my heart had stopped and that I hadn't been breathing, and that we ought to say a prayer of thanksgiving. Which I pretended to do with him, to be polite."

"Mouth-to-mouth?" said Sherry. "Was he cute?"

"Yeah. But his wife was in his canoe watching us the whole time."

Joyce stared at her. "Mal, I can't believe you never told me this story."

Mal shrugged. "It was a few years ago."

"A whole other lifetime?" said Joyce. "I mean, since you died and all."

"I guess you could say that."

"Damn," said Joe, with nervous impatience, and the other boys echoed him, giving less and less of a shit.

Ken's uncustomarily bright eyes stayed fixed on Mal until he was sure her story was finished. Then he jumped to his feet.

Spreading his arms, he boomed, "LADIES AND GENTLEMEN, ARE YOU READY FOR THE OPENING NIGHT OF OUR WHOREHOUSE?!"

The johns all raised whichever hand was not around their girls' shoulders and hooted. The girls raised their plastic cups of wine and said "Yeah," or "All right." Joyce felt Gregory's meaty hand tighten low on her shoulder. She remembered to be frightened.

"All right," said Ken. "I know you guys are in a hurry to, like, get your rocks off. And you girls want to get laid and get paid. But first I got to explain the rules of the house."

Sherry rolled her eyes ostentatiously and said to Joe, in a theatrical whisper, "He thinks he's really funny. . . ." *Watch out*, thought Joyce.

Ken gave Sherry a look. "I am." He reached into the back pocket of his jeans and pulled out that same rumpled, soft piece of paper. The customers watched as he laboriously unfolded it. "The rules of the house are all written on here," he explained.

Ken held the paper up close to his eyes, squinted at it, and made as if he were about to start reading. But he stopped, looked at them—his audience—held up a finger and said, "Just a second." Then he jumped into the next room, the kitchen. From her vantage point, Joyce could see him reaching behind the fridge and fiddling with something. "What the fuck?" muttered Phil, sounding as worried as he did pissed. Ken re-entered the room, holding propped on his shoulder the spiked bat. Joyce gasped to see it; it struck her oddly as a thing of true grandeur. Really, it was only a regular wooden baseball bat, a beat-up scruffy one, and through the fat end Ken really had driven a big rusty nail. Or, no, not a nail. A big rusty spike.

Gregory, Joe, and Phil all tensed. Maybe they thought they were about to be robbed without even getting fucked first. Or maybe they thought Ken was going to just start whaling on them with that thing for no reason.

Ken cleared his throat. He held the script up before his concentrating face with his left hand, and with his right held the spiked bat, displaying it. Back in character, he began.

"Gentleman. . . . Oh. There's a bunch of you. So gentlemen. Okay, start over. Gentlemen, you now see here in my hand a spiked bat." He held it up a little higher, for emphasis, then lowered it again, just as he had done in rehearsal. "In elementary school I was a star Little Leaguer, and in those days of yore I was oft known to knock the ball out of its cover, just like Robert Redford in that movie *The Natural*. Believe me, my friend, that gift has not been lost. If you are a good man, of true heart, like Launcelot in that movie *Excalibur*, then you need not fear me. But if ye be a Mordred, beware my lusty smiting. If you—"

"Yo, dude." The interruption came from Joe, spoken with a mixture of trepidation and annoyance. "Like . . . what is this, man?"

"Yeah," said Phil, "what the fuck, dude? Are you fucking with us or what? What is this shit?"

Ken lowered both speech and spiked bat and shook his head. "What do you mean, what is this? It's the speech, guys."

"Speech? What speech?" said Phil. Joyce noted that Gregory kept quiet, and decided that she had gotten the best of the three. The silence reflex was one she admired.

"My pimp speech," explained Ken.

"Your what?" said Phil. "Your fucking what?"

"Dude, don't use harsh language in front of the ladies. My pimp speech, man. What's to explain? I'm the pimp. I lay down the ground rules. I explain about our security procedures— which all y'all ought to be interested in, since they potentially involve the spiked bat. These procedures are detailed in the fucking pimp speech. Which y'all haven't heard yet. And nobody's fucking until this speech gets read."

"Uh." This from Joe. "Why don't you just *tell* us about these, uh . . . 'procedures'? What's up with the big long speech?"

Ken sneered. "I guess *somebody* never heard of *style*."

"Go ahead and wrap it up, Ken," Joyce said.

"No way. I'm not going to start again in the middle. The whole spell will be broken. I've got to start all over from the beginning."

Sherry made a vulgar noise deep in her nose. "I've *heard* it *before*. It's *not* much of a *spell*."

"Everybody's a critic. Look, nobody is screwing until I have satisfaction. This is my house and you're going to listen to me reading my pimp speech or else you're all going to go to a motel to fork over money for a room."

Phil was proving rowdier than Joyce had first guessed: "Dude, I'd rather do that than sit here and listen to some faggy bullshit."

"If you're going to a motel," Mal explained calmly, "you can do it without me. I don't know you. Ken, for better or for worse, is my pimp. He has that spiked bat for a reason: to wallop you if you fuck with me too hard. And there is no way I'm spreading it for some stranger unless he's within walloping range." After that, Phil only grumbled silently. You had to look at his face to see he was doing it.

Gregory shrugged. "Hey, I don't mind hearing some speech." Of course, Joyce thought, the poor trembling virginal dear; he would welcome a short reprieve before having to unveil his own merchandise. "I mean, it's not like we're on a schedule or anything." Joyce pursed her lips. In fact, a half-hour limit *had* been agreed upon, and reconfirmed several times. Apparently Ken had not bothered to mention this to their passengers on this maiden voyage. Or maybe Gregory had forgotten the rules in the heat of excitement. She studied his profile, his big soft square head. On his cheeks and chin were some rough patches he'd missed while shaving. Joyce didn't mind if today—a special occasion—they went a little long. "Just start over again, Ken," she said.

"All right." Once again he raised both paper and deadly bat, and, after again clearing his throat, began: "Gentlemen, you now see here in my hand a spiked bat." Again he raised it for clarification, then brought it down again. "In elementary school I was a star Little Leaguer, and in those days of yore I was oft known to knock the ball out of its cover, just like Robert Redford in that movie *The Natural*. Believe me, my friend, that gift has not been lost. If you are a good man, of true heart, like

Launcelot in that movie *Excalibur*, then you need not fear me. But if ye be a Mordred, beware my lusty smiting. If you are good, I will merely sit on this sofa and eat my cheesy poofs, avec docility. But should. . . ." He stopped, and raised his head like a rabbit sniffing for a fox. His audience froze, suddenly all newly aware of the sinfulness of what they were doing. Gregory cleared his own throat, a tiny sound. Joyce wondered if it was meant to camouflage a whimper. Sherry did not run her mouth, and tugged at her collar as if she were burning up. "What?" Mal asked, in a normal tone.

Ken raised a finger for silence. "I thought I heard something," he whispered.

Now Joyce knew he was screwing with them. Ken put down the spiked bat, leaning it gently against the wall, but held on to his speech as he walked to the window and stared out it. The glass was dirty, and it was dark outside, and all the lights inside the duplex were on, meaning he had zero visibility. "I thought I heard cops," he whispered.

Joyce groaned. Sherry muttered something not in keeping with the spirit of the game. "And what do cops sound like, doofus?" demanded Joyce.

"Like sirens, doofus," replied Ken.

"I don't hear no sirens," Joe offered helpfully.

"They were out there," Ken whispered, staring still and intently out the window. "They're still out there. I can feel it."

"Finish your fucking speech!" shouted Joyce.

Ken sighed and shook his head. "All these interruptions. It's damn unfortunate." He retrieved his spiked bat and resumed the position. Again he cleared his throat. "Gentlemen, you now see here in my hand a spiked bat." He raised it and lowered it. "In elementary school I was a star Little Leaguer, and in those—"

Phil howled. Joe said "Come *on*, dude!," while Gregory put his face in his free hand. "Don't start *over*, you asshole!" yelled Sherry.

Ken looked at them innocently. "I told you," he said. "The spell."

Despite her laughter, Joyce managed to say, "Dude, we are all so totally already under your spell, anyway. You don't have to start over. Really."

"If y'all were under my spell you wouldn't be laughing now. And now I've got to start all over *again*, because y'all interrupted me."

"Shit!" said Phil, but Mal hushed him. "Come on, Ken," Sherry pleaded, "*please!*"

Ken held out his hands and widened his eyes. "Hey, the more y'all cry, the less I care."

"Everybody shut up," Joyce commanded. "Let him finish and we can get to it." Sherry blanched, as if she'd forgotten just what Ken's antics had been delaying. Ken looked at Joyce with exaggerated gratitude and said, "*Thank* you."

"But no more fucking around, Ken," she said sternly. "Just read it through one time, and don't fuck with us again, or we'll all walk and that'll be the end of the brothel."

For her part, she was bluffing—but Sherry might soon start looking for a cop-out. So Ken gave Joyce a more straightforward nod and "Yeah" than she was used to receiving from him, and resumed his place where the TV ought to have been, once more holding the speech and spiked bat in their proper positions. "Gentlemen, you now see here in my hand a spiked bat." Raise, lower. "In elementary school I was a star Little Leaguer, and in those days of yore I was oft known to knock the ball out of its cover, just like Robert Redford in that movie *The Natural*. Believe me, my friend, that gift has not been lost. If you are a good man, of true heart, like Launcelot in that movie *Excalibur*, then you need not fear me. But if ye be a Mordred, beware my lusty smiting. If you are good, I will merely sit on this sofa and eat my cheesy poofs, avec docility. But should mine ears detect even a whimper of fear or horror from this nice young lady—uh, ladies—I will burst into the appropriate room like the wrath of God and wallop thee with this here spiked bat." Raise, lower. "Sir, I am but a small man. But lapse not into foolishness, for the spiked bat is a large man, and his throbbing instrument of both love and murder will seek out thy softest parts, to be sure.

To be sure, should you incur its wrath, never or rarely again will you suffer injuries more painful, or more embarrassing to explain to the police, or to your bodacious mom when you ask her for her credit card so you can pay off the doctor. That having been said, sir—uh, sirs—I hope that you shall sample our delicious wares with both honor and restraint, and cum and go in peace, so that we may remain friends and continue in this supercalifragilisticexpialidocious arrangement, or relationship." With that, he breathed a deep satisfied sigh and declared, "Let the fucking begin!"

Everyone looked at each other and laughed—everyone except Ken and Mal. Mal got to her feet first and extended a hand to Phil. He'd been planning some sort of chivalric gesture, but her offer caught him off-guard and he unthinkingly took her hand; she turned out to be stronger than anyone would have thought and hauled up a significant portion of the boy's weight, which took him by surprise and nearly knocked him off-balance. To Ken she said, "Remember that I'm taking the closet."

He nodded matter-of-factly. Joyce tried to identify this new facet of Ken: something like professionalism.

Sherry glued a hand to her hip and slanted her pelvis. "We haven't really *agreed* about that, though." Beside her, Joe jiggled on the balls of his feet. "I mean, why should *you* automatically get the room with the smallest cut?"

"Because I called dibs on it."

"But, yeah, but why should *you* get it?"

"Dibs."

"But why should *you* get dibs?"

"Because I called it."

"Well, that's not very fair."

"That's what dibs are."

"Well...."

"Listen. If it means so much to you, then you can wait until Phil and I are finished."

"Joe won't mind waiting!" hollered Phil. "But y'all're going to have to wait a mighty long time on *me*! *Haw haw haw haw!*"

Joe smiled and blushed and stared down at his Reeboks.

But Ken shook his head. "Nope, nope. All y'all go fuck at the same time," he said. "Otherwise I've got to spend extra time pimping. And I charge for overtime. If you make me work, like, twice as long, then I'll charge you double my biggest commission. That's just standard business procedures. Sherry, Mal has called permanent dibs on the closet."

"Permanent!"

"Come on," moaned Phil. "I swear, y'all're the fightingest bitches."

"I'll pay the extra," said Joe. Sherry took the hint and his hand and led him away.

Had they later had the whole thing on video, the girls would have laughed their asses off, maybe even Mal. Ken never exactly laughed his ass off, but he would have been unable to keep an occasional grin off his face, and would have provided hilarious narration. As it was, the girls and their johns lacked an audience and could not be their own, and so would never realize with what comical seriousness they went about their business that sinless, Edenic night (although Ken did gloat over their naiveté, like a big-city host with his country guests). The six tiptoed forth, through the tiny kitchen, to the back of the duplex. Like elephants or children they held hands, Joyce pulling Gregory pulling Sherry pulling Joe pulling Mal pulling Phil, who continued to haw-haw and did not pull Ken, who followed behind, a master chef seeing the meal all the way to the table. No one noticed that he was wringing his hands— until he himself did, and shoved them in his pockets. The overhead lights were off, the mattresses all had sheets, and, as a special touch, Ken had gone to Wal-Mart and bought a trio of matching gold (not real gold) bedside lamps, which he'd placed on the floor beside the mattresses.

They paused in Ken's bedroom and all stared at each other. "Well," said Sherry.

Mal was the first to make a move, dragging Phil to the closet. "All right, *baby*," leered Phil. She kicked off her

37

shoes before entering the closet, and Phil followed suit, like a monkey. "After you," Mal politely murmured. Seeming disoriented, Phil stepped in; even his first steps were of necessity onto the mattress. He appeared to realize only now that he was expected to fuck within the narrow confines of a walk-in closet. Mal followed him in, and turned to look at the rest of them one last time. Her face was grave, but she wiggled her eyebrows once as she said, "See y'all." Behind her, in his sock feet and ball cap, Phil turned in circles. "Is this *it*?" he said. When the door closed they heard him say, "*Yeah*, all *right*," and everyone but Ken laughed.

Joyce and Sherry looked at each other and, smiling, shrugged, forgetting for the moment the big friendly boys they had. Then Joyce led big puffy sweet Gregory to the marijuana room and closed the door behind them.

Sherry started leading Joe to the bed, then halted and narrowed her eyes at Ken, who stood there grinning with his arms folded over his chest. "You're *not* watching," she said.

"Okay, okay!" he said, raising his hands, "I'm going." Then he called out to all the girls: "So remember, if these guys get all rowdy and one of y'all needs the spiked bat, just let out a holler!"

From the marijuana room there was a grunt and Joyce's voice: "Okay!"

"But bear in mind that you might have to *really yell*, because I'm going to put some mood music on the stereo."

From the closet came Mal's voice: "Stereo?" Then Phil's: "Don't *worry* about it, baby." Ken left the bedroom, shutting the door behind him.

Sherry tilted her head back to get a decent look at Joe's face. He stared down at her with eyes wide and lips parted, sweat beads budding on his forehead, like he thought she was going to mug him. She slipped her hand under his untucked T-shirt and placed it flat against his belly; his abdomen felt like it was in the middle of a sit-up. It all suddenly seemed cute and vulnerable and under her power, and she smiled and said, "Well. Let's do it, I guess."

Meanwhile, as soon as the door shut behind them, Joyce hissed "*Get* in there, you!" at Gregory, then tumbled him into bed and dove after him. She started pulling his clothes off, and, when he tried to help, she grabbed his hands and forced them away, explaining that, as a paid professional, she would be in charge of everything.

"You can leave your cap on," she told him, when they were both pretty much peeled and she was straddling him.

"Th . . . that's okay," he said, but made no move to take it off. She had placed his hands firmly on the tops of her thighs and he was afraid to move them. "I don't mind . . . you know . . . taking it off. . . ."

"No," growled Joyce. "Don't take it off. It looks *awesome*."

Globetrotters. Café loiterers along the Champs D'Elysees. Volunteer ambulance drivers in World War One Italy. Movie stars, pop stars, and porn stars. The court of Louis Quatorze at Versailles. Neal Armstrong and Buzz Aldrin and Odysseus and Cortéz and Lewis and Clark and Hunter Thompson and all of them, the whole pack of them, the whole fucking pack of them—what did they—no, really—what did they—no, hang on, for real, this is serious—just what the fuck had they got that she didn't?!

And then, as she rocked on top of Gregory, Harry Mancini's "Moon River" began to blare through the house, and Joyce cracked up and paused for a moment. When they started again, she and Gregory tried to match their rhythm to the slow saccharine song's, and they actually managed pretty well. But Joyce had forgotten that Ken had two equally potent stereos (his mother, in most respects a frugal woman, had no sense of economy when it came to her Ken), until Funkadelic's *One Nation Under a Groove* came on, bass-heavy and strutting, duking it out with Mancini.

In their little room, Phil paused in his ministrations. "What the fuck is that?"

"That's the voice from the whirlwind, baby," said Mal.

"Do what?"

"Never mind."

Sherry was laughing about something cute Joe had said, when Ken burst in with the spiked bat. "Don't mind me!" he shouted, and, miraculously, they didn't. Sherry squealed and resumed her rocking as Ken executed a crude moonwalk across the room. "Hey, man, take a picture, take a picture!" cried Joe. Ken shouted, "Baby, what's my name?!"

"*Ken!*" shouted Joe and Sherry.

He moonwalked to the closet, flung open the door, brandished his spiked bat, and shouted, "Is everything okay in here?!"

Phil scowled over his shoulder at Ken, but his narrow pimply butt did not stop pumping. "Dude, you some kind of faggot or something?!" he shouted. "You come to see some shit?! This shit get you off?!"

"What?!" Ken shouted. "I can't hear you over the music! I just came to see if y'all were all right! I'm a pimp! I'm making my rounds! It's like being a waiter!"

"Do *what*?!" shouted Phil.

"A *waiter!*"

Mal tapped Phil on the shoulder and he returned his full attention to her. Ken, seeing nothing which did not please him, closed the door.

The glass rattled in the window frames. Ken had never turned the music up this loud, at least not both stereos at once. The speakers on the Funkadelic one were bound to blow, but, shit, fuck it! Resting the bat on one shoulder, he strutted again across the room where Sherry and Joe were still fucking, to the marijuana room door, which he threw open with a flourish, jumping in and declaring, "I've come, my sweet!" just as Joyce and Gregory were cumming. It was Joyce's first simultaneous orgasm, and Gregory's first orgasm ever with even one other person in the room. For Joyce, the quake came upon seeing her blurry pimp enter the room. "*HANG ON, KEN!*" she screamed.

Well, he was *well*-satisfied, Ken was, and he heaved a big, satisfied sigh and moseyed back to the living room. It was hard to sit in there, what with the jackhammering sound vibrations clogging the air, it was physically painful. But he managed not to turn down the volume. He let the Funkadelic album play out, one track after another, but he had "Moon River" programmed to repeat itself. As the song began for the sixth time, Ken became aware that the front door was being beaten upon. There was no sound, as such, at least not that Ken could discern; the music was way too loud for anything like that to get through. Rather, it was as if an extra set of steady, rhythmic vibrations had snuck into the room, and begun tickling the lobes of his reptilian brain. He opened the door to find two bemused cops, who asked him to turn the music down, please. He complied, with both stereos. Growing impatient, they asked if he'd mind turning one of them off completely. Ken sacrificed the Funkadelic, figuring that not only would the cops be slower to arrest someone listening to "Moon River," but also that it was a song they themselves would want to get away from. After checking his eyes for redness, they gave him a final, funny look, and asked him to keep it down for the rest of the night. They didn't ask if anyone else was around, or venture into the back of the duplex, where the girls had already finished wiping themselves off and were now sharing cigarettes with their clients. The smoke nearly suffocated Mal and Phil in their little closet, so they opened the door and, fumbling into their underwear, hung out with Joe and Sherry for a few minutes, before Joyce and Gregory joined them and they all drifted to the living room.

The guys paid up—three fifties each—with good-humored grins, saying, as they headed for the door, that it had all been worth it, and they were so totally going to come back. Of course, why should they give a shit about paying? It wasn't their money, it was their moms'.

The girls cheerfully told Ken that he'd get his cut after they'd scrounged up some change—no one had any little stuff at the moment. He smiled and nodded and said that was fine as long as in the end he actually did get paid, then got four bottles of Miller Lite out of the fridge and passed three of them to the girls.

There was a sofa, two armchairs, and a loveseat, but all four of them sat sprawled on the nasty carpet, leaning back against the furniture, pulling on their beers. Joyce was happily aware of the assload of money in her pocket. Then she laughed and said, "Hey Ken, you tell Melissa about your little side project yet?"

Ken shook his head somberly. "Naw. Discretion, remember? You tell her anything, the very next day it's all over the cheerleading squad."

Sherry gasped. "You mean you haven't told your *girlfriend* you're a *pimp*?!"

"Now, Sherry," he explained. "You know it's hardest for the children to understand these things. Is it such a crime for me to want to protect her from life's ugliness, just a little while longer? At least until I can get her trained to suck dick really well?"

"Your fault for being a cradle-robber," sniffed Sherry.

Mal eased a cigarette out of Sherry's pack, not bothering to ask first. "How is my old alma mater?" She cupped her hands over the flame of a lighter she'd found on the floor. "I drove by on Monday and all the whippersnappers were hanging around in front of the place. Too early to go home, too late for lunch. I figured it was a fire drill."

"Monday?" said Ken. "Monday was a bomb threat. Melissa told me."

"Oh, yeah? Just a prank call, or did they really blow the place up?"

"Does it matter?"

"I went to school there, too," said Sherry. "It wasn't all that bad. I mean, it sucked. But they're all the same, aren't they?"

Joyce had to take all that wonderful cash out again and just look at it. Holding it in her hands, she grinned and said, "Man, the thing is, I never came like that before. I mean, fuck the money. But I'm never going to fuck for free again."

Mal smiled back at her, took a drag off her cigarette and a swig of beer. "I never have," she said.

5.

That very night they decided to switch to screwing in the afternoons, since all of them finished classes early and this way their evenings would be free. Joyce and Sherry, of course, did not have jobs, while Mal had recently quit hers, at Kentucky Fried Chicken. "So I'm free from about two every day," she said. "I'll let you know how my schedule changes when I find a new job."

Joyce laughed and Ken dropped his jaw. Sherry glanced around, trying to figure out what was going on. "Are you kidding?" said Ken. "You just made a KFC's weekly paycheck! Cash!"

Mal shrugged. "More than that."

"So why would you go *back* to fast food?"

"What if I get sick of fucking?"

"Sorry. This is a dude you're talking to. Does not compute. And anyway, so what? Name one job that you wouldn't get sick of doing after long enough? By the way, I know it's harder for girls to have orgasms, and lots of guys don't even know there's a clitoris, and blah blah blah, but there's no way you'd get sick of fucking before you'd get sick of fry lamps. Anyway, bearing in mind that *one fuck* equals a week's wages, if you just bite your pillow and do it fifty-two times, you'll be able to retire for a year, no worries."

"I'm worried about the stability of our little venture."

"Stability? Dude, fucking may be the only thing you can guarantee. The oldest profession? Hello? It's not like the demand's going to die out. Shit, I'm thinking of fronting some cash myself."

"Mm. See, that's what I'm talking about."

"What?"

"It's not so much the stability of demand that makes me antsy, as it is of management."

Joyce butted in: "Ken was just kidding, Mal."

But Ken was grinning as if this were the perversely perfect cap to his perfect pimping debut. "Naw, that's okay," he said. "She's got good reasons to worry about me. But I promise to, you know. Not do anything to make it not be fun anymore."

Part of the reason they'd agreed to hold the sessions in the afternoons was that, as fun as opening night had been, they didn't expect it to be like that all the time. Unless they got the same three nice guys every day (which wouldn't happen—the johns would run out of money, Ken would become so disgustedly bored that he'd be forced to do something nasty in order to shake things up, and Joyce would insist on changing boys anyway because Ken would goad her into it by calling her a chicken), unless that happened, then at some point there was bound to be a dickhead in the mix, some jerk who would ordinarily be able to enrage them merely by hooting at them from a passing car, but who would be able, there, naked in a room with them and engaged in that most vulnerablizing of games, to leave them shattered for a good few hours. He'd grin and snarl and say "Flip over, whore," or something like that, and they'd yell at him, he'd yell back, Ken would come in brandishing his spiked bat, she'd demand payment even though he hadn't cum, he'd have something to say about that, and she'd storm off. Since the girls were sure that at least a couple such days must be in the cards, it made sense to get each session over with early. Otherwise, there would be a shadow hanging over every entire day.

What they'd failed to foresee, though, was that scheduling the debauchery for the middle of the day in itself made things less fun. An atmosphere of revelry was simply more difficult to attain between three and five in the afternoon. Joyce began to think that they probably ought to change the hours back. She was going to approach the others about it on their third day of fucking, but then, before the johns showed up, Sherry started gushing about this great new reality TV show she'd found, and about how glad she was that they were fucking in the afternoons, since otherwise she'd never get a chance to watch it. As usual, Sherry had to content herself with babbling to Joyce, since Mal and Ken pretty much ignored her, even going so far as to converse with each other instead, which rarely would have happened under normal circumstances. Joyce, faced with Sherry's breathless enthusiasm, didn't have the heart to rob her of her new nightly ritual, and so she kept her mouth shut.

Joyce started to worry about the word "cock." She worried she'd been saying it too much. Not that she'd noticed any such thing, but recently Ken had developed an impression of her in which he flung the word "cock" around brassily. Joyce had been bewildered, but it'd put Sherry in stitches and had even made Mal laugh, in such a way as to suggest that the imitation was pretty spot-on. So Joyce had brayed along with them, and secretly resolved to watch her mouth.

By the fourth day of screwing, Joyce had met neither the monster lurking in her future, nor Prince Charming (she figured a cathouse was as likely a place as any to find Prince Charming). At the moment her current mark, Floyd or something, had his pimply back to her, hunched over, deeply concentrating on something. Joyce suppressed a sigh. She wanted to ask him if there was anything he needed help with, but was warily reluctant because she wasn't sure she remembered his name. Could it actually be Floyd? It couldn't, could it? Was that still a real name? They were naked in the marijuana room. She was stretched out on the mattress—fully-sheeted, she'd made sure. Floyd or whoever had rolled off when, in the middle of a garlicky kiss, she had tugged the elastic waistband of his boxers down past his bony hips. He'd snapped them the rest of the way off himself, and had been huddled there on his side ever since, hunkered down in a vaguely ominous way. Joyce cleared her throat and simply said "Hey," unwilling to risk calling him the wrong name, especially a wrong name like Floyd. "Hey, baby. What's up?"

He didn't reply. A real charmer. Then again, that was the whole point of getting a whore, was not needing to charm anyone. That didn't give him the right to bore her to death, though. "Hey," she repeated. "Anything I can help you with?" Then, when he didn't say anything, she added, "I am a professional, you know."

Floyd or whoever grunted in response. Or it could have been a word of some kind. "Excuse me?" said Joyce.

"Just a second," he mumbled. He didn't seem to be in a bad mood, or any mood at all.

"Okay," Joyce said dubiously. "I mean . . . if you're sure it's…?"

"Hang on," he said. "Just let me get this on."

"Oh, *that*!" Joyce exclaimed. What a dummy. Of course! "Oh, I can help you with *that*!"

"No, I can do it. Just a second."

"Aw, come on," she said. Then, in what was supposed to be an alluring sing-song: "I can make it *fu-un*."

"No! I don't want you to see it."

Both her smile and belly froze. "Why not?" she demanded.

"Because," said Floyd or whoever. Despite his distant mildness, there was a new stubbornness in his voice. Maybe he was just embarrassed, but Joyce had been stupid for having forgotten to look him over: a visual check on all penises was one of their rules. Condom or no, she didn't want some herpetic cock knocking around in there.

"Let me see."

"No. I'm almost done."

"Let me see it. Now. While you're still bareback."

"Jeez, what's the problem all of a sudden? Hold up."

"Let me *see* it!"

"Fuck off!"

But she'd already hopped around him and pulled his scrawny arms and hands away. He offered all the resistance of a half-reanimated corpse, and once overpowered he averted his bulging froggy eyes, his zitty chinless face.

Joyce looked at his cock. It lay there like a dead fish on the floor of a boat. Peremptorily and primly, like a nurse, she lifted it, checking its underside, rolling back the foreskin, fingering through the pubic hair as if she were on a lice safari. Everything seemed decent. A discolored patch gave her pause, but she quickly determined that it was only a birthmark. So what had been the big deal? Why had this goober put up such a struggle? Then she grasped the obvious: Floyd was flaccid.

She looked up at him. "Aw, were you embarrassed to let me see you like this?"

Floyd or whoever did not answer, but Joyce could see his eyes had welled up, and now a tear spilled out onto his cratered cheek.

In spite of her cynical affectations and aspirations, the sight of boys crying sent Joyce into a near-panic and caused her chest to go all airless and gaspy. "*Uh*-uh," she said, clutching his shoulders and pulling herself to him urgently. "Don't you *worry*, honey."

Floyd or whoever wiped the tears away with the back of his fist. "I'm *going*," he said, and made as if to rise.

"*Uh*-uh!" repeated Joyce, pushing him down again. "Now, you listen, sweetheart. There is just no fucking way. You hear me? No fucking way. Now, we are in the back room of the house, which means we don't have to worry about anybody else traipsing through, which means we can take as long as we want. You hear? Now, I'm willing to go extra innings on this, free of charge. All right? Are you with me?"

Floyd or whoever thought it over. Finally, he nodded.

Later, an exhausted Joyce followed her ecstatic john out of the marijuana room, her good deed done for the day. Once Floyd or whoever had skipped out the door, she plopped onto the armchair and joined Mal and Sherry for a beer. Ken was on the floor, laboriously practicing his scales on an out-of-tune guitar. "How'd y'all do?" Joyce asked the other girls.

"Don't ask," said Mal. "How about you? You were in there so long, I thought he'd knocked you up and you were having the baby already."

"He just needed guidance. What do you mean, don't ask?"

"I had some frat boy. Big muscly fuck. You saw him."

"Yeah."

"Well, he turned out to be a real comedian."

"He made fun of you?"

"Shit no. He was more like a real old-fashioned sort of comedian. Like a ventriloquist."

"Okay. I guess I'll just, like, sit here and wait patiently for you to get around to whatever the fuck you're talking about."

"He was a ventriloquist and his dick was the puppet. He made his little urethra-hole move like a mouth while he did a comedy routine in this high-pitched buzzy voice."

In the second before Joyce started to laugh, Sherry gave her a disgusted look and said, "Isn't that gross?" Joyce said, "You mean he uses his hands?"

"Of course he uses his hands."

"What was his routine like?"

"Oh, you know. What would you expect from a dickhead like that? 'Hey, baby, you got your snakebite kit? I sure hope so! Huh-uhuh-uh-uh!' That kind of shit."

Ken looked up from his twangy guitar. "But, hey, that's not bad."

"Shut up, Ken," Joyce said cheerfully.

"Sherry had a good day," Ken said. "Ask her. Sherry fell in *love.*" Joyce looked at Sherry as Ken tauntingly said "*Oooo*" and Sherry blushed and squirmed, struggling to hold back a smile. With a shock Joyce realized that Ken might be right, as far as Sherry was concerned, anyway. "What's this?" she asked.

"Nothing," Sherry said. "Of course I'm not in love with any of the boys we're fucking, don't be stupid. He was just nice, is all."

"He was pretty nice," Mal agreed. As usual her face was clear, and seemed free of dissembling. "Unless he was faking." Sherry shot Mal a grateful look.

Mercifully for Sherry, the conversation then moved away from her john, who was named Bryce, and whom she reckoned

48

she might really be in love with. He'd shown up at the same time as Floyd or whoever and Dick-Puppet, but he hadn't known them. Sherry, Joyce, and Mal leaned against a wall while the johns sat on the sofa, looking confused, as Ken stood over them, holding that dumb spiked bat, reading that weird speech. Bryce was the one in the middle, though Sherry didn't know his name yet. What a dork he was. His body was a skinny bundle of sticks. On top of his neck was balanced a very round, pale head, like a big ball; his red hair was slicked down and somehow plastered to his scalp, so as to accentuate the roundness. He had a beaky nose and nonexistent lips. His watery blue eyes were small and uncertain behind the thick lenses of his black square-framed glasses. He wore a long-sleeve gray-black-and-blue button-up shirt, tucked into the tight blue jeans that hung loose on him, with a brown belt that matched his brown pair of nice walking shoes. Finally, Ken had finished his silly speech, the johns had stood up, and Ken had introduced everyone, announcing all six names. Sherry had stepped forward and, taking Bryce's hand in hers, said, "Dibs."

In Ken's bedroom she'd spoken to him in whispers, and he'd responded to her discretion with his own low tones. Delighted, she'd run her finger down his red treasure trail. "Is this really your first time?"

He'd seemed decently embarrassed. "Yes."

"How come you decided to come to the brothel?"

"It was sort of a spur of the moment thing. That guy Ken just asked me. Half the reason I came was to see if he was being for real."

"Uh-huh. What about the other half?"

"I thought that I ought to get some experience. So that when I meet the girl of my dreams, I don't embarrass myself."

"That's a nice idea."

"I don't know." He'd gulped, but otherwise maintained his composure. "Now I'm thinking maybe I should have gotten the experience earlier. Because what if you're the girl of my dreams?"

"Aw," she'd said. "You're doing just fine."

Bryce appeared to be the nicest john they'd ever had, and Sherry considered it a triumph that she had scooped him up. Afterwards, she'd urged him to come back, and he had said he would try. Then she'd whispered that she would try to get him a discount—a big one. But that, she'd warned him, was super-secret.

6.

For a week all the johns were assholes. Mal got Dick-Puppet again, plus a guy who got rowdy when he was refused a lap dance. "I don't do shit that makes me feel stupid," she explained calmly. He made a stink for a while, but when Mal told him that he could take it or leave it, he sullenly allowed himself to be fucked. Mal didn't much care what they were like, as long as they paid; and they all did, with nary a whine. Ken's spiked bat had turned out to be as persuasive as he'd promised.

Meanwhile, Joyce suffered her own petty humiliations. First, a guy who kept slapping her on the hips and buttocks, muttering "Come on, bitch, come on," in some tedious Dirk Diggler fantasy; Joyce counted her teeth with the tip of her tongue, waiting for Superfly to hurry and splooge. He might just as well have gone out to a field and found a nice fat cow. Somewhat creepier was this frat guy, Atchley. Joyce already disliked frat guys, especially in the boudoir. Even so, it was difficult to put her finger on exactly why Atchley immediately scared her so much. Something about the jokes he told. Plus he wore a Sig Tau shirt; those guys had almost gotten their charter revoked, because a gang of them had broken into the house of a rival frat and beaten its members with flashlights. In the room, taking off their clothes, Joyce felt convinced that there was something off-kilter about the guy. Once naked, Atchley had trouble getting it up. He accepted some help from Joyce, but mostly insisted on working it out himself. All the while a big grin was smeared across his face. The grin frightened her: he was unashamed of his impotence because nobody was there, really, to see his performance. Joyce didn't count.... That was the vibe she got, anyway. The fucking itself was fine. She just couldn't relax during it, was all. Afterward he yuk-yukked and asked Ken if he could get a discount because she'd had a huge nasty fucking pimple on her butt, and once the door was shut behind him, she hissed at Ken never to invite him again.

Sherry's week went better, but she was still put out because two of her johns asked her to stop talking while she fucked them. One asked her politely, but the other just told her to shut up. Not only that, but a couple of johns heaved big sighs right in the middle of her stories, after they'd been riding her for ten minutes or so.

But unbeknownst to the rest of the gang, Sherry had a consolation prize: Bryce. He had taken her out twice so far, once to dinner and a movie, once just to dinner. He was a perfect gentleman, never getting fresh, only giving her a peck on the cheek when he dropped her off at the dorm—God, *she* was fresher than he was! He said that for their next time he wanted everything to be perfect. He said that having been so ignoble as to pay for sex would have been the worst mistake of his life, if he hadn't been so lucky as to have chanced upon her. Bryce said a lot of sweet things, and at restaurants he pulled her chair out for her. He did look like a total dork, but even that was sort of charming (not that Sherry thought with words like "charming." She thought he was "cute").

They still had classes and stuff, and Joyce remembered that she had an exam coming up in Dr. Morgenthau's World Lit class. She'd done crappily in the class to date, and hadn't read any of *Candide*, or the book before that, whatever it had been. Some poetry thing. So she decided to pay a visit to the prof, because his exams always included exhaustive essay questions (a thousand words or less), and nothing could convince Joyce that the grading of these essays was not an entirely and scandalously subjective process. Therefore, she figured that a personal show of interest, a reinforcement of the face which matched the name, might be enough to push Dr. Morgenthau's evaluation of her essay into a friendlier spot on the critical spectrum. She'd perused a classmate's notes just enough to manage an intelligible question about *Candide*, and now she walked down the carpeted blue-and-gray hall of the English building to Morgenthau's office. She rapped on the doorframe, a grin already fixed on her face, and, as there were no other students present and the professor was there reading a book at his desk, she stepped inside, automatically pulling the door closed behind her.

Dr. Morgenthau glanced up and greeted her with a vague smile. Then, once he'd placed her, his expression darkened. "Would you mind leaving the door open, please?"

Joyce hesitated. Lots of the male professors left their office doors wide open when they had female students inside, and there were rumors of professors recording all their meetings, in case of any accusations. Had Joyce been thinking, she wouldn't have closed the door. Even so, it was odd that Dr. Morgenthau should worry about such things. He had no wedding ring, in every work they read he managed to find a gay character, and it was widely assumed that he was a homosexual himself. If Joyce were to tell any of her classmates that Dr. Morgenthau had hit on her, she'd be laughed at. But she supposed the university lawyers wouldn't laugh; nor would her mom and step-father consider the news that one of her profs was gay much of a comfort. Fair enough. "Sorry," she said as she opened the door, trying to give her most professionally innocent smile. Then, with just a hint that Dr. Morgenthau had overreacted: "Guess I wasn't thinking."

Dr. Morgenthau leaned back and steepled his fingers. "That's fine," he said. "Joyce, right?"

"Yeah," she said, pleased that he'd remembered her name, considering she'd never raised her hand in class.

"I thought so. What can I help you with?"

"Uh . . . well . . . it's just, I sort of had a question about the book, you know. You know, for the test."

"I know about the exam, yes. Which book? There's been more than one, I'm sure you're aware."

Joyce tried to laugh, and wound up yelping like the prof had pulled a gun on her. "*Candide*, sir." Jesus, since when had she called the fucking professors "sir"? "I had a question about *Candide*."

"All right. Shoot."

"Well, uh, there's that woman. You know? Cunegonde's maid, I think. The one who gets half her butt eaten by the starving guys in the boat. You know?"

"Yes. I know. I first read the book when I was twelve, and I've been teaching it now for fourteen years."

"Oh. I guess so, yeah. Well, I was just wondering. You know how, like, when we talked about that book in class, it was like all the different parts meant something? Like, they all had some special meaning. So I was wondering if all that stuff about her getting her butt eaten off was the same way. Like, when you read it, it's so funny, you don't think about anything else. It's just . . . you know . . . funny. But it's also pretty horrible, when you stop and think about it. I mean, it's a pretty messed-up thing to do to somebody. So, I guess I was just wondering, since it's like all funny and horrible all at the same time, if it had some special meaning, like the rest of the book. Or, uh . . . if it was just funny." She shrugged to signal that she was done. Shit. Stupid lame bitch. She should have looked over those notes better.

Dr. Morgenthau waited, as if not understanding that she'd finished. Then, seeming at a loss, he spread his hands and said, "If you're looking for some specific metaphorical or allegorical meaning, that's open to interpretation. I suppose that perhaps Voltaire is telling us something about the nature of humans, who will eat the living flesh of their fellow creature without compunction. On the other hand, yes, certainly it's meant to be funny."

Joyce nodded, as if this were very profound and she had to give herself a moment to let it sink in. She tried to think of a graceful exit line. Dummy! Dr. Morgenthau would remember her, all right. "Okay," she said, "thanks a lot, that really helps."

She spun around in retreat. But Dr. Morgenthau called her

back. She jerked to a halt and half-turned to face him, one foot still edging toward the door: "Mm-hm?"

He studied her, head tilted back and to one side. At last he said, "Do you know a guy who calls himself Ken?"

And here she'd been priding herself on her recent strides towards unflappability. She'd held eye contact with Mal. She'd smiled and put a calm hand on her cool hip when Ken had done things that could have gotten the both of them seriously fucked up. Despite her middle-class background and total lack of addiction expenses or cash flow problems, she'd fucked many strangers for money. And all it took was her nice World Lit professor confronting her with Ken's name to make her blush, fast, hard, and crimson. She tried to salvage the situation with a bright, friendly, probably maniacal grin, which Dr. Morgenthau was in no mood for:

"*Do* you?" he repeated.

Joyce nodded enthusiastically, as if they were making fun small talk. "Yeah, I know Ken."

"Are you aware that he came to see me earlier today?"

"Nope, I didn't know that."

"Would you care to venture a guess as to what he wanted to talk about?"

She burst out laughing, and exclaimed, "Oh, I could guess, but no, I wouldn't want to!"

Dr. Morgenthau's eyes narrowed. "What exactly does *that* mean?"

Joyce let her laughter trickle away. Having started with her big super-watt smile, she felt stuck with it now. She shrugged. "Nothing. Except that Ken has a kind of oystery sense of humor."

"Oystery?" He sounded annoyed rather than curious.

"It's an acquired taste."

"Oh. Yes, I suppose so. He had some rather unsavory propositions."

She kept grinning, desperately willing Dr. Morgenthau to see it all as a big joke. "I can imagine. But he's just a big kidder."

"All of these propositions involved you."

"Well, you know. We're buddies. We kid each other a lot. He was probably just playing a practical joke on me and he took it too far, is all."

"This was the kind of kidding that could get him sued for slander. Assuming he's lying."

"You know, I was just the other day watching a TV special on how America's being crippled by needless litigation."

"His 'practical joke' wasn't entirely limited to you. He saw fit to make me a part of it, too. I believe his guarantee was that you would—how did he put it—'turn' me. Or my money back." Now would have been a good time to quit smiling. She didn't, but on the inside her face fell. Earlier in the semester, some jock in the back row had demanded to know "how come all the books we got to read up in here are full of faggots?!" Dr. Morgenthau had continued with the lecture, but grimly ordered the jock to see him after class. Now Joyce felt like someone more qualified should be called in to give the professor a hug. For her part, she just kept grinning stupidly at him. Later she would realize that he must have thought she was laughing at the joke.

Once it was clear that her expression wasn't going to change, Dr. Morgenthau shook his head and returned to the papers on the desk. "I don't appreciate being harassed on account of my sexuality. I said as much to your little friend, but I'd appreciate it if you could reinforce the message. . . . What's more, I don't enjoy having the details of my students' unsavory pastimes graphically related to me during my work hours." Shooting Joyce a look, he added, "Whether they're true or not." She kept on grinning like a wax woman. "Please tell 'Ken' that if there's a repeat performance I won't hesitate to lodge a complaint with the university authorities. I'll feel no qualms about mentioning your name as well."

Joyce finally jettisoned her ridiculous grin. In what was meant to be a conciliatory tone, she said, "I'm sure Ken was only kidding, Dr. Morgenthau."

Her effort to make up didn't put a dent in Dr. Morgenthau's cold armor, not after he'd had to stare at that funhouse grin.

No wonder—since junior high, how many hours had she spent staring into mirrors and practicing looking smug? Without looking up, Dr. Morgenthau said, "Yes. He didn't seem to take much of anything seriously." Joyce shrugged, offered a weak goodbye, shuffled out of his office, and hurried out of the building. Although she'd dropped the smile, the blush was harder to shake.

But it was gone by the time she got to the brothel. For one thing, Joyce would never show Ken even a speck of squeamishness if she could help it. She was planning to confront him right away—although she would've been hard-pressed to say why, since she couldn't confess to any anger, and had in fact almost convinced herself that she wasn't even really mad about his little joke, although it was too bad Dr. Morgenthau had gotten miffed. But Sherry had arrived at the brothel first, and was in the middle of declaiming one of her never-ending anecdotes at Ken. She was standing in front of him, arms straight down at her sides, bent forward at the waist, head pushed out, blue eyes bulging out of her reddening face, her strident tones growing more and more insistent as the story progressed. Ken looked away, picking imaginary bits of something out of his hair and pretending to eat them, ignoring Sherry. When Joyce entered, Ken looked up at her with cartoonish relief, and, removing a thumbnail from between his teeth, stepped toward her with his arms out. "Thank *God* you're here," he exclaimed, "I have had *no* one to hang out with—"

"*Ken!*" shouted Sherry. "I am *talking to you!* . . ." Luckily, Sherry's john for the night was Bryce, and even luckier, he showed up early. Joyce yielded them the marijuana room over Ken's protests, so that they wouldn't have to worry about Joyce and her tardy john traipsing through. Ken turned to Joyce and, while Sherry and Bryce were still in the room, said, "Well, Joyce, *you* don't have to pay the higher percentage." But Sherry was so happy to see Bryce, and Bryce was so embarrassed to be in the living room of the brothel with everyone knowing what he was about to do, that no objection was raised.

Once Ken had read the speech and the couple had left the room, he stared after them, shaking his head. "I don't know," he said. "I don't like it when my girls get too attached to one client. Bad for business."

Joyce confronted him about the Morgenthau incident, which he readily took credit for. They had a good laugh over it. "Yeah," said Ken, "he got pretty pissed when I brought up the whole gay thing. Go figure. I was like, dude, I don't care if you fuck boys, I'm just saying, don't you want to *try* fucking a girl?"

"Reasonable."

"I thought so. And I pointed out that since I was offering him his own student, he already knew the goods were good. I was like, hey man, don't be a fool. That Joyce is a fox!"

"Much obliged. I wonder what he got all fussy about."

"Go figure. Some people, you know? Oh, and he got all touchy when I started in about where he was from, too."

"Where he's from? He's from Mabelvale, I think."

"Naw, naw. That name, I mean. Morgenthau. Sounds like he's Jewish. Or German. Or German-Jewish. Or something."

"Ken, you make such poetry out of ignorance."

"Well, what else am I supposed to do with it?"

Just then Joyce's john showed up. Ken read the poor guy the spiked bat speech, even though it was like his fourth time to hear it. Then he waved at them as Joyce led the guy back to Ken's bedroom to get fucked. They didn't talk about the Morgenthau incident again.

7.

A boy who sat next to Joyce in World History told her about a party that was being thrown by a friend of a friend of a friend of his. He drew her a map; the house was comfortably outside the town limits. There would be assloads of alcohol, he assured her, though it was always a good idea to bring your own, as there were bound to be still greater assloads of people. This boy seemed to have no idea that Joyce was a whore. Joyce told Mal, Sherry, and Ken, none of whom had anything better to do on Saturday night. (Sherry made a sassy joke about how it wasn't like they had to get up for church on Sunday morning, and Joyce and Mal smiled politely.) Somewhere along the way, the three whores and their pimp had become each other's primary social group.

Ken had the richest parents and the biggest car, so he drove. They parked near the house on a swampy patch of ground, with other jumbled cars of every age and description: classic muscle cars, a Lexus, beat-up pick-ups, shiny girlish pick-ups, a Chevette that would still chug along in earnest frailty, secondhand Hondas, a VW van with dolphins grotesquely airbrushed onto its sides. The place was pandemonium, with music thumping through the night air to scare the crickets, people shouting and shrieking, and the light of a bonfire on the other side of the house haloing it and diffusing out from its edges. Most of the guests were college-aged, but a few stretched out into middle age, and, after a bit of detective work, they found that their host was, in fact, a hostess—a fifteen-year-old sophomore at Conway High who was dating a junior at CAU, and whose parents were out of town for the weekend. Joyce went on reconnaissance and, after asking around, reported back to the other three that their benefactress was buck-naked and drunk in the bathroom upstairs, lying in the tub and squealing with delight as her boyfriend and his buddies dumped cooler after cooler of ice into the water to see how much she could take. Apparently the chick was planning on having all the mess cleaned up by the time her parents got back tomorrow night. They had a big laugh at the nasty surprise that would welcome her when she came to.

The girls naturally had no problems getting drinks, and Ken was able to smooth-talk his way into bumming one apiece from each girl's supplier. They did have a cooler stuffed with beer in Ken's car, but no one felt like fetching it—they'd have to contend with parasites bumming off of them, and the heavy cooler would require constant guarding. They parted ways for a bit. Ken wandered off to try to get laid, Melissa not being quite trained up yet (although he'd assured Joyce that she was getting there, moving around more and all that), and Sherry, with vague, inexplicable haughtiness, informed the girls that she was going to go mingle. Joyce and Mal stayed together by default. Mal asked Joyce what she'd been doing with the extra money the brothel brought in. Joyce shrugged. "Oh, you know. I'm not really in it for the money."

"You been putting it in the bank?"

"No, I guess it's still lying around the room."

"Like in a shoebox, under the mattress? Or maybe that's not the sort of thing you should tell your roommate."

"Jesus, like I give a shit. It's not in any hiding place. It's just kind of spread out through the room."

"Are you sure? I haven't seen a bunch of cash lying around. I'd notice if there was like a thousand dollars on the floor."

"Well, it's all still balled up in the pockets of my dirty clothes. I actually haven't done laundry since we started the whole brothel thing, you know."

"See, that's what comes of too many clothes. Makes you soft and lazy."

"Fuck off."

Sherry drifted back. Soon Ken rejoined them too, having managed to become flushed, red-eyed, and sweaty. Sherry threw up her arms: "*Excuse* me. I thought you were supposed to be the designated *driver*."

Ken took another pull off his beer bottle. "Yeah, sure, no problem."

"But you're drinking! You're drunk!"

"I'm buzzed. But I'll be drunk soon, yeah."

"But you're the designated *driver*!"

"Yeah, I know. I'm the one designated to drive. Okay. I agree to drive. But I never said what condition I was going to drive in."

Sherry stared at him, eyes bugging out. Then she spun around and flounced off to mingle some more.

Ken wiped his mouth on the back of his hand. "Bet you I could take her out back and fuck her."

Joyce smirked. "That'd be a neat trick."

"Not so neat." Ken turned to Mal. "How you doing, Mal?"

She'd crossed her arms. "I'm cool."

Ken wandered back into the bowels of the big house, stalking whatever havoc was there to be wreaked. Although there seemed to be no prohibitions on smoking indoors, Mal and Joyce stepped out onto the porch with their cigarettes. There had been a porch light, but someone had smashed the bulb. It was a clear night, and this far out in the country there were actually stars, bushels of them spangling the sky. Mal said, "There's trouble brewing between Ken and Sherry."

"Yeah, I know. Neither one of them seems much interested in making things easier."

"Well, Ken knows he has nothing to be scared of. Soon it's going to blow up. It'll take our little venture with it, too. I figure that's the only reason Ken's been holding back."

"Well. If Sherry dropped out, I don't see why you and me couldn't keep going. That's the way Ken wanted it originally anyway."

"But Sherry won't just go. She'll stay and let herself be tortured until she's totally fucked up. I don't think Ken'll resist torturing her much longer. And it'll be a big noisy unpleasant process."

"Oh. Yeah, that too. . . . So what're you saying? We ought to get day jobs?"

"You don't need a job."

"I know. I was just kidding." Then, a little shyly, she said, "You need a job, though, don't you?"

"I've already got one."

"What? You mean the brothel?"

"No. A real one. I work nights, since we're doing the fucking in the afternoon."

"What job? Since when?"

"Three days ago. I work over at Foxy's."

"Foxy's?"

"That strip club just off I-30, right after you leave Faulkner County."

"Holy fuck. I've driven past it before, but I've never. . . . What do you do there?"

"I'm an electrician."

"What? Really?"

"No, not really. I'm a stripper."

"Wow."

"I'd been playing with the idea before the brothel started. And I decided to go ahead so I'd have something to fall back on when the shit hits the fan with those two and it stops being worth the headaches. It's no big deal. I guess actual whoring is a baptism by fire as far as sex work goes."

"What was the interview like?"

"I danced naked for the boss during off-hours."

"What music did you dance to?"

"Something awful. I didn't know it."

"Can you bring your own music?"

"They said I could. But why bother?"

"This is so cool. Do you have a stage name and shit?"

"Yeah. Lilith."

Joyce laughed. "Does anyone get it?"

"Nobody's seemed to yet."

"Yeah, I guess they wouldn't. Bunch of redneck farmers and truckers."

"Oh, no. They're not all country people. There're all kinds of guys in there. Every sort."

"Still. You ought to do a strip-tease to Sarah McLachlan or one of those other Lilith Fair women. That'd be bizarre."

"No. I'm not that MTV, Wiccan Lilith. I'm the old Lilith, the Kabbalah Lilith, the one who flies through the desert and'll fuck you to death."

Joyce didn't know what the Kabbalah was. She took out a fresh cigarette and lit it off her old one. "Dude, I can't believe you've been a stripper for three days and didn't tell me yet. I mean, we see each other every day."

Mal just looked at her. She said nothing.

They would have changed the subject anyway, but crashes and screams from within the house did it for them. The girls hurried inside, and came to a halt when they saw Ken lying on the floor on top of a smashed coffee table, blood trickling from his nose, trying to catch his breath because he was laughing so hard. Over him loomed a huge frat boy with bunched fists. Joyce recognized the Greek letters on his shirt—Sig Tau, the same fraternity as that creepy Atchley. The Sig Tau scowled down at Ken. "Keep laughing, faggot." Ken obeyed. "Keep it up."

Other frat brothers advanced out of the crowd, fists equally clenched, and soon there were four of them towering over Ken. Mercifully Atchley was not one of them—maybe he was upstairs, laughing at the whiteheads on some twelve-year-old girl's butt. Joyce wondered what Ken had said to trigger his beating. She also wondered if they ought to interfere, Ken being their friend, nominally. But they were girls, which probably offered them an out. Joyce decided to take her cues from Mal, and glanced over to check her reaction. Mal was watching impassively. So Joyce did the same, for now.

The lead frat guy grew neither more nor less ominous. He might have seemed stuck in stasis, except for the threats that continued to leak out of him. "You think it's funny?" was what he was saying now. "You think it's fucking funny, punk? Huh? Huh? Do you?"

"Yeah," Ken cheerfully confessed, and started to work his way back up to his feet. The frat boy and his goons watched his struggle with sullen clay eyes. Joyce felt acid roiling in her stomach, because if one of these thugs kicked Ken in his ribs or something while he was regaining his feet, her pride wasn't going to let her play the gender card. She would have to march over there and actually try to punch somebody.

But the quartet remained stone-still and gorgonized, almost like gentlemen, as Ken rose. He kept weirdly laughing. So did the crowd; the four frat boys, Joyce, and Mal seemed the only silent ones in the house. Most jeered and hooted, thrilled or amused by the imminent spectacle. Joyce saw Sherry on the other side of the ring that had formed around the combatants. Ken's latest snub (and doubtless a thousand others) was still fresh in her mind, and she'd had enough beer and wine coolers to forget herself. Now her face twisted and spat as she howled for Ken's ass, looking like a savage Goldilocks at a bear-baiting.

Ken was standing again. Instead of assuming a defensive or combative position, he stretched, pulling his arms high up over his head and standing on his tip-toes, all the while laughing in the frat boys' faces. The leader of the quartet curled his lip back like a bizarro Elvis and said, "What're you laughing at?"

Ken sighed and shook his head at the boy affectionately. Then, shockingly fast, he bent over and reached out and swooped up one of the broken table legs, and when he came upright again he leaned it jauntily against his shoulder. Jagged splinters of wood projected from the broken end of the thing, and Joyce nearly gasped to see how like the spiked bat this makeshift club looked. Many in the audience really did gasp, and the frat boys jumped back, startled for a moment. Pride and public opinion, though, would not let them off the hook. They eyed him warily.

Ken swung the table leg suddenly, but then, instead of striking anyone, he popped its smooth, still-varnished bottom end into his mouth, thick as that wood was, and began to jerk it slightly and rapidly back and forth, pantomiming fellatio, moaning muffled through the wood, screwing up his eyes, gyrating his hips and with his free hand clutching his penis ecstatically through his jeans. The spectators, after a brief quiet moment of adjustment, erupted. There was laughter, but for the most part the reaction was a cacophony of angry howls and disgusted, indignant protests, along with a fair bit of fake retching. Joyce's innards crumpled—surely Ken had crossed some sort of line somewhere. He might even get himself killed, this time. She glanced at Mal, who had lit a new cigarette and was coolly watching with her arms crossed.

The frat boy—the leader, the original one—could hear the hungry cruel righteousness of the mob, could see that it was now or never, and indeed that the kismet of bloodlust ordained that it must needs be now, and so he stepped forward, muttering "You fucking faggot" (not that anyone could hear him over the commotion), reaching out to swat that indecorous stick from Ken's hand. Ken was facing this frat boy, which also meant that the table leg pointed directly from Ken's mouth to the frat guy's nose. As the guy drew close, Ken suddenly, and with great force, jerked the table leg straight out of his mouth and thrust it forward along an invisible rail, burying the ragged splintery end in the boy's nose with a loud crunch. The boy screamed and everyone else hushed. There was that unreal shock that accompanies a person's first glimpse of a movie star in the flesh. The frat boy's deputies lurched forward. They were bigger than they were fast. Ken, holding the table leg now like a baseball bat, hauled off and hit the guy on the left flank in his left ear with the blood-speckled broken end, leaving a welt along his jaw. The guy on the right he took out with an uppercut, swinging the club up into his chin with something akin to a golf stroke, except with a really short golf club. There was a little cloudburst of blood then, raining up. Joyce caught another glimpse of Sherry across the way, screaming with her eyes wide in horror. The middle deputy, having had time to observe the threat so unexpectedly posed by this faggot, managed to land two quite respectable, heavy punches on Ken's face. Unfortunately for him, Ken was by this time pretty much plumb crazy, and too adrenalized to notice any setbacks shy of vivisection. He walloped his opponent once with the table leg, but the angle was bad and it was only a glancing blow that didn't do much damage. What did work, though, was the kick to the nuts. Once Ken had his adversary doubled up, he began to pummel the guy's beefy face with the club.

Joyce shook herself and decided it was time to get the fuck out of Dodge before somebody really did kill Ken. Had it occurred to her to wonder whether Ken *ought* to be saved, she might have paused long enough for anything to have happened. But she was running on reflexes. Grabbing Mal's upper arm—it would have been the hand, but Mal's arms were still crossed and so her hands were tucked in behind her elbows—she shouted "Come on!" and dragged her colleague along with her into the arena. Mal rolled with it. Joyce grabbed Ken's arm and again yelled "Come on!" She didn't expect any cooperation from him— God knows what might have happened if she hadn't gotten it, since, glancing across the room at the staircase, she saw a whole platoon of well-fed white boys hustling down, faces hard and swollen with affronted murder, looking down at the carnage and, it seemed, at her. Most of them wore those same Sig Tau shirts. When Ken saw them pouring down the stairs there was a small tug of resistance on Joyce's hand as he paused and happily exclaimed "*Ho,* boy!" But he allowed Joyce to yank him out of the house. They ran for the car. Ken kept almost stumbling, and, seeing how drunk he was, Mal demanded his keys, which he handed to her in mid-stride. From behind them came outraged half-articulated howls. Luckily, Ken's parents were rich enough that his car had electronic door locks with a remote control on the key ring, meaning that when they got to it they were all able to tumble in right away. Had it been Joyce behind the wheel, they would have lost precious seconds while her hands shook too violently to fit the key into the ignition—had it been Ken he would have wasted time doing something funny and dumb until they got a rock through the windshield—Mal slid the key into the ignition as if she were a robot built for the purpose, started the engine, and switched on the headlights. Those frat boys really were running after them, screaming. One of them had a wooden stick that he was waving overhead like a crazy person. Mal moved the car three inches in first one direction, then another, until it was plain that, thanks to some bad parking jobs, they had been hemmed in. The bloody shrieking frat guys drew nearer. Mal said "Sorry" and slammed on the accelerator, bashing her way through the too-narrow gap left by the two cars in front of them, smashing Ken's right headlight and making a horrid screeching noise. For a vomitous moment Joyce thought they were going to be stuck there, but the swampy ground was soft enough that Mal was able to shove the other two cars a bit to each side as the paint came screaming off all three of them. Then they popped out like a cork, the frat guys jumped out of the way, and Mal fishtailed around to the road. Behind them, for just a second, they could hear the frat boys jeering at them over the damage to Ken's car—the guys apparently assumed that, just because the car was expensive, someone would care about it.

Mal drove fast the first minute or so, just in case they were in for a car chase. Then she slowed down. Joyce forced her hands to steady themselves and lit herself a cigarette. Only after she'd already taken two puffs did she think to roll down the window. When she pressed the button to do so, a cold blast of wind buffeted the right side of her face, and she jumped, as if she hadn't been expecting it. "Can I have a cigarette?" asked Mal. After Joyce passed her one, she said, "Thanks."

Ken was sprawled in the backseat, arms spread out and head leaned back, silent and meditative. Before the two front windows were rolled down, Joyce had been able to hear his breathing, which had not been rapid, shallow gasps, but satisfied intakes and releases of air. Now, without raising his head, he spoke up, strong enough to be heard over the steady roar of the wind. "We have to go back," he said.

Joyce ground her teeth and stared out the window, ashamed of her cowardice. Mal said, "You can drive yourself back after Joyce and I are at the dorm."

"Aw. Party-pooper. Anyway, I'm too drunk to drive. Just ask Joyce. I bet she'll say so."

Joyce laughed and let out a cheer. "Fuck, Ken, I don't think you've ever been too drunk to do *anything*."

"But we got to go back. We got to go pick up Sherry."

"I think she'll get along without us," said Joyce sarcastically. Mal did not deign to reply.

"Naw, really," Ken said. The patch of space before them that was illuminated by the headlight seemed very small. "I mean, what am I going to say to Sherry? The next time I see her?"

8.

The damage to the car was no big deal. Ken told his mom that it had been swiped for a joyride and later found in its current state, keys dangling from the ignition. Nah, dusting for prints wouldn't do any good—without thinking, he'd gone ahead and put his hands all over the keys and steering wheel and everything. Anyway, there'd probably been a thousand people in and out of that car, each one leaving his or her fingerprints behind. Mom knew what a popular guy he was. Despite scolding him a little for being too trusting and open-hearted, his mother showed a great deal of sympathy when he called to let her know about the whole thing, and insisted that Ken borrow her car while his own was in the shop. She and his father could make do with just one. When she dropped the vehicle off, she was horrified to see his swollen black eye. But Ken gallantly refused to divulge the culprit's name, explaining that it was a good friend who had gotten drunk and then forcefully resisted Ken's (eventually successful) efforts to drive him home, and who had since manfully and copiously apologized.

The girls arrived at Ken's place for work two days later, just like always. Right before the sessions began, a tearful Bryce showed up, and Sherry had to be called out to get rid of him. After a heated conversation in the front yard, eye-rollingly observed by Ken through the window, still-weepy Bryce was persuaded to leave, and Sherry came back in, teary-eyed herself. She granted her john a sullen and distracted fuck that wasn't worth the money.

That first day back Joyce kept watching Ken and Sherry for some sign of extra tension, Sherry having so recently screamed for his blood. But there was nothing. Well, Ken did grab Sherry's boob and give her a mild titty twister, sending her into a short screaming fury, but that was all in a day's work for Ken. And Sherry, for some reason, did casually ask Joyce for the full name of Ken's little high school girlfriend. Joyce automatically gave it to her, and afterward felt vaguely stupid for having done so.

The next working day Joyce had to be a half-hour late because she had her mid-term conference with Dr. Morgenthau. Ken made a stink about it, but Joyce insisted it couldn't be helped. The conference was routine, so much so that Joyce had the eerie sense that their previous, fraught meeting had never happened. Joyce was doing okay but Dr. Morgenthau knew she could do better, etc. When she got to Ken's, Atchley was sitting on the loveseat, palms resting on his spread knees. Mal and Sherry were noisily fucking in the back part of the house, so there was no question of switching johns with either of them. Atchley leered at her and said, "How much for you to blow me, bitch?"

Ken was sitting cross-legged on the floor, the spiked bat leaning back against one shoulder, the crumpled notebook paper in his hand looking more and more the worse for wear as the weeks went on. He jumped to his feet and said, "Cool, let's get started," and took his position and began to read in his monotone: "Gentlemen, you see here in my hands a spiked—"

"Come *here*, Ken," Joyce snapped, marching past Atchley to grab Ken and pull him into the kitchen. There was no privacy, with only a thin wall and no door separating them from the john, but Joyce felt a psychological comfort from being in a different room. "I'm just going to have to start the speech over again," protested Ken.

"What the fuck do you think you're doing?" Joyce hissed.

"Pimping."

"God damn it, Ken. God damn you. I told you last time. *Not this guy.*"

Ken screwed up his face in consternation. "Why not? He pays his bills."

70

"He's fucked up!" Although this was the first time Joyce had ever been obviously and undisguisedly mad at him, Ken showed no surprise, no distress, no amusement, no reaction at all other than that fake puzzlement. "I fucking told you last time, Ken. He scares me. There's something wrong with him."

"Like what? Does he want you to wear a wig and granny panties and a breast pump?"

"It's nothing I can put my finger on. Okay? I'm just scared of him. There. Are you happy? You win. Just get rid of him."

"You know, he can so totally hear every word we say. This is not the way to get yourself a fat tip."

"Fuck yourself. Get rid of him."

"You are so chicken."

"Gobble gobble. I mean, cock-a- . . . oh, fuck it."

"You're acting like a girl, dude."

"Hear me roar. Just get rid of him."

"Listen to me. Will you just listen to me? What am I? What's my job? Have you or have you not heard my brilliant spiked bat speech?"

Joyce groaned.

"Well, have you ever *listened*? Come on, Joyce, I'm a pimp. It's a joke, but it's also true. I mean every goddamn word of that speech, and the day one of y'all do have to let out a holler is the day you're going to see me shine."

"Well, I don't much like the idea of seeing some guy's brains splattered all over the wall, either."

"I doubt I would ever have to give anyone a literal whack. I figure just the presence of that bat all swinging around should be enough to stop anyone from getting too frisky."

"What if it's not, though?"

"So what? I'll give them the elephant gun treatment."

"I don't *want* to see anyone get the elephant gun treatment. Don't you understand that?"

"Bullshit," said Ken, and started to laugh. "Naw, dude, I don't understand that at all. Now don't chicken out on me."

"Quit calling me a chicken."

71

"How about quitter? Didn't you say your step-dad called you a quitter? Like, when you dropped Astronomy?"

"Fuck off."

"Come on, Joyce. I thought we were going to show them."

Feeling herself slipping, Joyce tried to make light: "I figure I've already shown half the guys on campus."

"Since when is half enough?!" Ken cried. "Come on. You started this thing with me and I'm fucking counting on you. Don't chicken out on me now. Don't get fucking complacent. Don't get ordinary. Let's take this thing to the next level."

Arms crossed and standing contrapposto, she eyed him dubiously. Even though he was about an inch shorter than her, she had the weirdest impression that she was looking up at him. "All right. What's this 'next level' of yours?"

Ken pointed excitedly at the wall, on the other side of which was Atchley, perhaps a foot distant from Ken's finger. "Walking back in there, letting me read my spiked bat speech, then walking that guy back into the weed room—hopefully before Mal gets done in mine, so you can walk through there while they're still going at it and like so totally heighten the effect—walking him back to the weed room and fucking him, after he's been sitting in there listening to us talk about how much you hate him, and how I'll fucking tear him up if he makes you holler—dude, *that's* the next level. For starters, anyway."

Joyce bit the insides of her lips to keep from smiling. "Explain that."

"I don't need to explain shit and you know it. That shit is self-ex-fucking-planatory. Dude, Joyce, that would be *living*. You could retire after some shit like that, if you could stand to. You'd've already stored up a whole shitload of treasure in Heaven and you know it."

Joyce couldn't help it any longer—a grin broke out across her face.

Ken grinned too, in triumph and relief. "That a girl."

"I'm laughing at you, freak."

"Big deal. You're still in."

"I can't let you pack your bags and run off to crazy without me, can I?"

Atchley hadn't moved; his pose proved that it was possible to swagger while sitting down. He sneered at them, and especially at Joyce, while she did a pretty respectable job of meeting his gaze with equal scorn, and mixing in some sultriness. Ken read out his spiked bat speech. Then Joyce led Atchley—who was very tall—back to the marijuana room. Usually Joyce led her johns by the hand, but not in Atchley's case. She didn't even turn over her shoulder to smile invitingly, or sway her hips as she sauntered ahead of him. Nor did she check to make sure he wasn't up to any funny business. In Ken's bedroom, Mal was riding the hell out of some guy like he was an electric bull. The sheets had fallen away, so they could see pretty much all of Mal, along with the jiggly top half of the chubby john. Joyce knew that all the effort she was putting in must mean that the guy wouldn't cum. Mal paused as Joyce and Atchley walked through the room. She grabbed a burning cigarette from the ashtray on the bedside table and, after a quick glance at Atchley's leer, which seemed calculated to give maximum offense, she looked Joyce in the eyes. Beneath her, the john timidly protested: "Hey, what're you guys doing in here . . . hey, don't *stop*. . . ." Everybody ignored him. From the closet could be heard the sounds of more fucking. Joyce said, "What's up? I thought you had permanent dibs on the closet."

Mal shrugged and exhaled a cloud of smoke. "We got off to a late start, and we knew you'd turn up before we were done. And you know how Sherry doesn't really like to be looked at. So she threatened to walk if you were going to come through before she finished."

"Fair enough," said Joyce, and took another step towards the marijuana room.

"Hey, hold up," said Mal. She looked at her john with very mild surprise. "Don't *you* go away," she admonished, and wagged her hips back and forth a few times to keep him primed. Then, after another glance at Atchley, she said, "Ken's fucking with you, huh?"

Joyce grimaced as if to say that she was an old sly dog herself, but yes.

"Just let out a yell if there's any trouble. Ken's an unreliable dick, but he won't be unreliable about that. If you yell, he'll come and hit this guy with that thing."

"Shit, I know that. It's his job." She glanced derisively back at Atchley and led him the rest of the way into the marijuana room, while Mal ground out her cigarette and got back to work.

The lonely mattress had fresh sheets. Ken had been surprisingly good about that sort of thing. Joyce left it to Atchley to shut the door behind them, which he did, roughly. She kicked off her sneakers, then unzipped her jeans and pulled them and her panties off at the same time, with her back to Atchley so as to moon him when she bent over. She turned around, still in her socks and sweater. "You got your own condom?" she said.

"Yeah," said Atchley. "Ain't you going to finish getting undressed?"

"Naw. I don't feel fucking romantic enough."

"Shit, bitch, you like to play too, huh."

"Blah blah, tough guy. Why don't you just go ahead and wrap up your little needle cock so we can get this over with."

"Bitch, I said, ain't you going to finish getting undressed?"

"Nice to see you're more like a regular asshole this week, without all the weird dumb jokes."

"My jokes are funny, bitch. Answer my question."

"I already did, jackass. Why? Can you not get hard as it is?"

"I wanted to nut all over your fat titties, is all."

"Tough titty. You pay for pussy, you get pussy. Nothing else."

"That's fine." He undid his pants, took out his erect penis. Joyce looked at its swollen reddish-purple head and forced herself to smirk. Atchley took out his wallet and got a condom out of it, which he unwrapped and began to roll onto himself. "I got me a big rubber spermicide wall to protect me from all your nasty jungle juice, bitch." Joyce rolled her eyes. He continued: "Shit, I kind of like the idea of you staying dressed. Why should I have to look at your nasty fucking fat body?"

Joyce walked over to the windowsill, where the room's supply of KY Jelly was kept, and applied a handful to herself in a businesslike way. Dully, she said, "You want bottom or top?"

Naturally Atchley wanted the top. He fucked her obnoxiously, one claw pinching the bone of her pelvis and the other rammed up her sweater to squeeze her tit. He hadn't gotten undressed either, and he grinned and sweated down into her face. The bill of his cap, which he also had not taken off, kept whacking her in the forehead and nose. Joyce gazed coolly over his shoulder, trying to look bored and vaguely disgusted and unhurt. It was the face she sometimes used to punish guys, to send them back to flaccidity so that she could then rescue them, and teach them that they needed her (that was always her plan, anyway). With Atchley, though, it seemed to have the opposite effect. Fine. Whatever. He certainly didn't seem like the great-lover type, at least, which meant he'd probably finish up pretty quick. He sure had last time, mercifully.

But then he stopped abruptly. Joyce snapped a hostile glare onto his face. He was grinning down at her. "You want me to hurt you?" he whispered.

"What?" She loaded the word with all the derision she could muster.

"You heard me, bitch. You want me to hurt you? Like, *really* hurt you? Fucking break your nose or rip your nipple off?"

Joyce snorted. "You're pretty dumb if you can't remember the fucking spiked bat speech after having heard it twice."

"Oh, I remember it. Your little pimp with the baseball bat with the nail in it who's going to smack my brains out the second you call him." Atchley whispered, "Call him."

"You're nuts," said Joyce.

"Uh-huh." He tightened the claw on her hip. Joyce struggled to break loose but couldn't. "I'm nuts, so you better call him. Miss Smarty Pants." The pain in her hip became so intense that an involuntary little whimper broke free.

Atchley looked gratified. He eased the pressure. Joyce refused to look grateful. Then she noticed the spit bubbles rapidly multiplying at the midpoint of Atchley's lips. "You better not," she had time to say, before the spit landed right in the corner of her left eye and she had to squeeze it shut against the sudden burning. "Call your pimp," said Atchley.

Joyce was on the verge of doing exactly that, but then, horrified, she stopped herself. Suddenly she saw the whole deal: if she cried out, Ken would be true to his word, all right—he'd rush in to bury that nail somewhere in Atchley's flesh. And Atchley was just as ready for a showdown. Ken and Atchley, in their mutual hunger, had somehow found each other in the cosmic current, and she was to be the medium of their conflagration. Ken was no doubt waiting by the door of his bedroom, squeezing the handle of his wooden bat with hot slippery palms. There had been no plan between the boys, no spoken conspiracy. But Ken knew that Atchley would hurt her because he would have recognized it in Atchley's face, and Atchley knew that Ken would burst into the room swinging his spiked bat because he would have seen it in Ken's. . . . Well, Joyce had no desire to have the penis of the apocalypse within her. Nor did she want to be sprayed with Atchley's blood. So she would keep it to herself and they could go kill each other on their own time. She spat, "Go ahead and fuck me and get it over with."

He laughed as cruelly as he could manage, but Joyce heard his disappointment. Later she would try to squeeze some satisfaction out of that. Anyway, he did at least go ahead and fuck her quick and get it over with. He was rough, but there was nothing barring that in the contract (i.e., the spiked bat speech to whose conditions Atchley had tacitly assented), so Joyce was able to preserve some pride and pretend that what had happened had not happened. When it was all over, she went to the bathroom to wash her face. Reclining nude on the mattress, Atchley called, "What, I got to sit here and wait for you to wash that shit off your face?" He was talking about her tears.

"Fuck off," she answered over her shoulder.

She forced herself to be tough and not shut and lock the door as she bent over the sink and washed her face in the crisp cold water. She wanted very much to get some clothes on, but she wasn't going to give him the satisfaction of seeing her hurry. "It's going to take an awful lot of washing to make *you* presentable," he called. This time she ignored him. When they finally dressed, she saw that he was smirking; then his shirt slid over his face.

Sherry and Mal had finished fucking, and the duplex was quiet except for the sounds of Ken puttering around in the living room. But a tear-streaked Sherry was waiting on the loveseat, while Ken sat on the floor and idly flipped through his CDs, ostentatiously not looking at her. "All right," he muttered, without looking up at anyone, "Joyce is done finally, you can fucking go now." It was impossible to guess how much of his bad mood was due to Sherry's extended presence, and how much from his missed chance to really use the spiked bat. As soon as she saw Joyce walk in, Sherry sprang up from the loveseat and hurried to her, blue eyes sticky and red-rimmed, her hands folded between her breasts. Without glancing at the departing Atchley, Sherry loudly whispered, "Joyce, can I talk to you outside?"

Joyce hesitated and glanced down at the back of Ken's head. Oh, he deserved so much shit. But maybe it was for the best that Sherry was here to distract her. Screaming at Ken was unlikely to provoke a very satisfying response—not satisfying to her, at any rate. She shrugged and said, "Yeah, sure." As the girls left, Joyce said, "Bye, Ken," and got an uninterested "Bye" in return.

It was a clear day. The green leaves against the blue sky looked sort of yearning. Even the cracked and peeling white paint of Ken's duplex had a certain loveliness in this light. The girls stood facing each other in the front yard. Joyce folded her arms and said, "What's wrong?," perhaps more brusquely than she'd meant to.

Wiping away a fresh tear, Sherry said, "I've really had a lot of fun, hanging out with you guys at the brothel, Joyce."

Joyce waited. This in itself did not seem like something to cry over.

"I mean, I don't even care about the money. You know I'm okay for money. It was just . . . it was just about being one of the girls, you know? And about being on this big crazy adventure."

"Yeah, I know."

"And, Joyce. The girls I wanted to be one of was really just you. Not so much Mal and Ken. You know that, right?"

Joyce widened her eyes. She opened her mouth and closed it. "Wow. Thanks, Sherry."

"It's true, swear to God. That's why I wanted to talk to just you about this. And not those others."

"Okay. Talk about what, Sherry."

Sherry took a few seconds to work up steam. "Well," she began, and then the words came rushing out: "Well, I guess you know I've been seeing that one guy Bryce outside of work? Like, we haven't even been fucking except in the brothel, which we only did a couple times and then stopped, even though when we did it it was really nice. We've just been going out on these really gentlemanly dates where there's only kissing, and even then only at the end, or else maybe during the boring parts in the movies . . . and he, like, says that he loves me, Joyce, which is nuts but he cries and looks like he means it, and also he says he'll stick by me even if I decide to keep on fucking at the brothel but he really wishes I'd quit."

Sherry paused, either to catch her breath or else to give Joyce a chance to respond. Joyce found it nearly impossible to remain impassive—not so much at the revelation that Sherry and Bryce had embarked upon an affair, but at the news that sensible-looking Bryce had so quickly professed his love for the rich spoiled whore he'd happened upon. Ah, the mysteries of the human heart. All hail the harvester of virginities. She blinked and said, "Really?"

Sherry nodded. "And I've always told him that I couldn't stop. That I was, you know, like, *finding* myself. That I couldn't sell out so easy. And actually, Joyce, I so totally love the whole *fellowship* thing. Like, especially between you and me. The *sisterhood.* And that's why I didn't feel like I could just up and quit fucking the guys here."

"I know what you mean. So what's changed?"

"Well, I was in there, you know, in the closet. And there was this big boy on top of me. And all of a sudden it was like I couldn't stop thinking of Bryce, and of those couple or three times when we did it, and how much nicer it'd been than it was with this great big boy, and how much I want to like marry him and do that again and have babies. Marry Bryce, I mean, not that big boy. You know what I mean?"

"Sure." At least they would be getting rid of Sherry and the blowup between her and Ken might be avoided after all. Joyce's nerves were still raw, and all this fuck-talk creeped her out. Instead of merely crossing her arms, she now hugged herself, rubbing her upper arms to keep warm enough to stop her shivering. She kept glancing over her shoulders and out of the corners of her eyes. "I'm happy for you."

Sherry burst with relief: "*Are* you?" she said, beaming.

"Yeah, sure. Totally."

"But, Joyce, really, I meant everything I just said about being in the brothel. I feel so much less . . . *scared.* And so much more *alive.*"

"It sure is a great big crazy experience."

"You can so totally say that again. And that's sort of why I wanted to ask you if I could still hang out here. Even if I'm not fucking."

Joyce could have sworn that her face fell, except that Sherry didn't seem to register anything. "But why would you want to hang out at the brothel if you weren't fucking anybody? I mean, when me and Mal're in the back, you'll just be sitting there with Ken. And y'all hate each other."

"Just to feel like a part of things. Anyway, I can handle *Ken.*"

Joyce let this wild assertion pass. "What about Bryce? Won't he still object to you being in a place that's so . . . you know . . . unwholesome?"

Sherry earnestly and violently shook her head. "Oh, *no.*

Bryce knows that I'm not, like, a hothouse *flower*. He wants me to be my own *woman*. And he trusts me to just hang out here. If I tell him I didn't do anything, he'll *believe* me." Now her eyes widened in appeal. "Please, though. If you say it's all right for me to hang out there, then Ken and Mal'll fall in line. But if you sort of, like, withhold your *blessing*. . . ." And Sherry waited, holding her breath, to see if this calamity would come to pass.

It had been a shit of a day and Joyce didn't give a shit about what Sherry did anyway. "Hey, man, whatever you want to do, you know? I can't tell you where you can and can't go, right?"

Sherry flung her arms around Joyce's neck and squeezed her close. "Thank you!" she exclaimed. When they stepped back from each other, Joyce saw a cartoonishly sly look on the reformed hooker's face. Sherry said, "And it'll give me a chance to get back at Ken for that titty-twister bullshit. Or, like, I mean, to watch when he finds out . . . you know . . . what I've done."

"Sherry, please. Just let it go. For real."

Sherry laughed and waved her hand with oh-you dismissiveness. "Don't worry! I can handle myself. Anyway, I'll see you back here tomorrow. I already told Ken not to book anybody for me." She put her hand over her mouth to stifle a giggle. "I can't wait to see his face when he finds out I'm coming anyway as a spectator!"

But Joyce was already shaking her head. "Uh-uh," she said firmly. "Tomorrow's a day off. You mean the day after."

9.

The day after next, Mal and Sherry were already in the living room when Joyce arrived. The door was wide open and there was no sign of Ken or any johns. Joyce frowned and peered around the room, as if Ken might be hiding behind the furniture. Mal was sitting cross-legged in the armchair, smoking a cigarette, looking annoyed. "What's up?" asked Joyce.

Mal ashed her cigarette in a dirty saucer. "We got here, the door was open, the place was deserted. I figure I can give him about half an hour. Any longer and I'll be late to Foxy's."

"Well, Ken could be up to just about anything." She plopped down beside Sherry on the loveseat. Then it struck her that Sherry appeared remarkably pleased with herself. "What's up with you?"

Sherry held up her palms in a show of innocence. "What do you mean, Joyce?" she asked sweetly.

Mal looked Sherry up and down in an unimpressed way. "I've already asked her. She won't give."

"I have no idea what y'all're talking about," Sherry assured them.

Joyce felt some foreboding, but with savage bitterness told herself that it wasn't worth worrying over, and turned to Mal. "You mind bumming me a cigarette?"

Mal pulled out a cigarette and tossed it to her, then sent the lighter sailing after. Joyce had a feeling that Mal had indeed minded, but had seen no advantage in stirring up shit by saying so. The vibe made Joyce feel heavy and wish that she hadn't asked for the smoke after all. Here it was, though. It would be silly and weird to return it. She lit the cigarette and tossed the lighter back. Last week she had bought a pretty wristwatch at Wal-Mart with her earnings. She checked it now, partly because she was interested in the time, partly to again admire its pretty face. Secretly she hoped that Ken would stand them up, him and whatever johns he may or may not have rounded up. A part of her hoped Ken was dead.

But such was not yet to be. After a few minutes he walked in, nodding hello to all of them. There were no customers with him.

Mal crushed her cigarette in the saucer. "So are we fucking anybody today, or can I go back to the dorm and relax a little before I go to work?"

"Oh, there's guys coming. I just pushed the time back by half an hour. I hope that's all right."

Mal said, "It's all right with me, but I won't be here when your friends show up. If I stick around that long I might be late to Foxy's. You'll have to fuck them yourself."

"Well, I'll ask them, but I wouldn't be surprised if they weren't down with buggery. These are some pretty good Christian boys, you know. Nothing but the best for my girls." Ken turned to Sherry. "You think you could help us out? Come out of retirement for a one-night-only gig?"

Sherry looked very smug and proper. "I'm afraid not. You should have thought of all those little details before you changed the schedule without telling anyone."

Ken shook his head in a show of remorse. "I know it," he confessed. "I know it. It's just that I'm a little off-kilter right now. See, I had some heartache yesterday. But Sherry can probably explain all that shit to you. Can't you, Sherry?"

"Fuck," said Joyce. "Goddammit, Sherry, what've you done?"

Sherry had been busy attempting to combine an innocent gaze with a gloating leer—now she looked startled and uncertain. Mal had apparently decided to stick around for a while, as she'd lit a fresh cigarette and was gazing coolly at Sherry, who flexed her jaw and said, "Why don't you ask Ken?"

Ken was leaning back against the window, elbows resting on the sill, feet planted where the TV should have been, studying

Sherry as he spoke to the other two. "Y'all know my girlfriend Melissa, right? Anyway, you do, Joyce. And then I came to find out yesterday that Sherry does, too. You know, Melissa's called me a lot of names. But yesterday she called me something that I figure she must have had to look up in a thesaurus first. I'm, like, so proud to have increased her vocab."

Mal, bored, said, "What did she call you?"

"Whoremonger," said Ken.

Joyce groaned.

"What?" Sherry demanded. "It's *true*, isn't it? She had a right to *know*, didn't she?"

"Jesus, Sherry," said Joyce. "You didn't just tell on *Ken*. You told on *us*! You told on *me*!"

Sherry paled. But instead of apologizing or even conceding the point, she placed her hands tightly on her knees and faced forward. "*You* would want to know. Imagine if it was your boyfriend, and especially if you were just a *high* school girl. Imagine how she would have felt if she'd found out later, by accident."

"I don't give a shit how some stranger might have felt," said Joyce. "I just care about what you did to *me*!"

Ken shrugged and went on: "So me and Melissa are through, which is too bad because I'd just got her up to where she could suck a decent dick. Now she's going to go off into the world and suck some loafer's dick, and he'll get all the fruits of my fucking labor. That'll be my blow job he's getting."

Still not looking at anybody, Sherry primly said, "Well, you just should have thought about that."

Ken waved his hands, as if to say that that was neither here nor there. "I guess I can't complain too much about people telling the truth, even if I personally don't see much point in it. The thing is, though, Melissa also 'found out' that I was cheating on her."

"You're not?" asked Mal with mild surprise.

"Well. She was under the impression that I was doing it *regularly*, and with a very specific person. A certain blonde-

83

haired, blue-eyed, voluptuous whore." He compressed his lips and shook his head, disheartened by the wicked behavior all around him. "Now, I don't know where she could have gotten *that* idea."

All eyes turned to Sherry, who raised her chin and actually closed her eyes as she haughtily explained, "I believe what I said was that you had been *coming on* to me."

Ken showed no emotion. "I'm still in the dark here," he said.

Sherry made it clear by her face that his weaseling was pathetic. "The *groping*?"

"Uh-huh," said Ken. "Well. Okay. I'll see if I can work with that. Um . . . I'm groping for your *meaning*. Is that what you're trying to say?"

"Everyone in this room has seen you feel me up."

Ken looked from Joyce to Mal. "I guess I throw myself upon the mercy of the court," he said. "Witnesses?"

Mal looked right at Sherry and said, "I don't know what you're talking about."

Sherry stared open-mouthed at Mal. Then, her eyes welling up, she turned to Joyce in appeal.

"No," said Joyce. "Sorry, Sherry." Really, though, she wasn't, as her clipped tone made clear. "If you're being serious you'd better explain what you mean."

Sherry stared at her, truly uncomprehending. "He felt me *up*." She whispered, because her words were meant for Joyce, and because she was ashamed. Even so, Mal and Ken could easily hear everything she said. "On my *boob*. You were *there*."

Joyce stared back. Finally she said, "Are you talking about the titty-twister?"

There was a sharp snap of mirthless laughter from Mal, and Ken slapped his hand on his forehead and left it there a while, his head tilted back. Joyce laughed too. "What?" demanded Sherry, humiliated and furious. "*What?*"

"Never mind," Ken said, "all's forgiven or whatever. I can see how someone could make a mistake like that, if they were the same type of person as Sherry."

"It's not a *mistake*, motherfucker!"

But Ken was already walking out of the room. As he went, he said, "Hey, y'all stick around, I want to show you something."

"I'm going to go hang out in my dorm room before I go to work, Ken," said Mal.

"Naw, hold up, trust me," called Ken from the depths of the apartment. "It'll either be fun or interesting, I promise."

"No," said Mal, and stubbed out her cigarette. "No more *bullshit*, man!" Joyce felt both satisfaction and fear at seeing Ken get to *her*.

Ken popped his head back into the room from the kitchen. "Come on. Stick around. This'll only take a few minutes. And if you miss it, you'll just want to be filled in later." He snatched his head back and was gone.

Mal pursed her lips as she gazed at the wall. Then she lit another cigarette.

Sherry sat with her knees tight together. "He *did* feel me up. He put his *hand* on my *breast*."

Wearily, Joyce said, "It's not the same thing, Sherry." Her mind was elsewhere. It had only just occurred to her to wonder if Atchley had actually raped her. Not legally, of course. If he had raped her, it seemed to follow that Ken had raped her, too. She hoped to discredit that notion before her friend-cum-pimp re-entered the room. . . . Could she have somehow raped herself?

Sherry wouldn't leave the whole titty-twister thing alone. "Well, why isn't it the same thing?"

Joyce spread her hands. "It just isn't." Mal continued to smoke and silently, expressionlessly watch them both.

Ken came back into the room with an old black tape recorder. "Guess what," he said, "I figured out how to record telephone conversations this morning."

"Oh yeah?" said Joyce, speaking only because she knew that if Ken were met with silence, he would go off on some massive tangential "joke" about them not replying. "Who'd you call?"

He peered at her with faux suspicion. "Who says I've called anyone, huh?" Slumping deeper into the loveseat, she groaned. "Just joshing with you," Ken said. "I'll let y'all listen for yourselves." He pushed the play button on the machine—a fuzzy hiss filled the room. Ken stood like a schoolchild giving a recitation, but with the tape player instead of his mouth. His hands were clasped before his crotch, and from those hands hung the black tape player. They heard the hum of a ring tone. It was surreal to hear such a normally intimate, ear-cupped sound, magnified so. There was a rattle, then a sleepy, disembodied voice: "Hello?" Joyce noticed that Mal was studying Sherry.

Ken's voice followed, although for a split-second it was difficult to identify it through the distortions of the machine. He addressed the callee respectfully by his surname, preceded by a "Mister." Joyce had never heard him do that with anyone before, and she knew that this man, whoever he was, was in for it. Then she realized that the surname was the same as Sherry's.

They heard the man say, "This is he."

"Hi," said Ken. He could sound so pleasant. "I'm a friend of Sherry's. You're Sherry's dad, right?"

"That's right."

"Oh, good. I've been trying to reach you for a while now. There are lots of people in the Little Rock phonebook with your same last name, you know. I called, like, three of them before I realized that I only needed to call people in the nice neighborhoods. Pretty stupid, huh?"

Sherry's dad sounded annoyed. "Who is this?"

"Uh, I told you. I'm a friend of Sherry's up at CAU. Actually, sir, it's Sherry I've called to talk to you about."

"Is Sherry in some sort of trouble?"

"Oh, well, you know. Define 'trouble.' *Moral* trouble, for sure, if you count that sort of thing. Which I assume you do, because I've heard y'all're such devout Christians. The rest of the family, I mean, not Sherry so much."

Now Sherry's dad was awake and pissed. "Sherry is every bit as religious as. . . . Who the hell is this, anyway? How dare you call me up and say these kinds of things about my daughter? What's your name?"

"Hey, man, I may be a stranger to you, but Sherry knows me. I'm her pimp."

"You're her what?"

"Her pimp, man, her pimp. Sherry fucks strange dudes for a living."

Sherry seemed to have departed from the realm of normal time, her mouth forming a slow-motion silent scream. Joyce was on the verge of telling Ken to turn off the tape player when the conversation was picked back up and Joyce shut her mouth, like a rabbit shutting its eyes to hide. "What did you just say about my daughter?" asked Sherry's dad in a soft, dangerous voice.

"Dude, keep up. I said she's, like, a whore, and I pimp for her. I recruit the guys she fucks and I also do security. It's interesting work, you know. Not exactly what I had in mind when I picked my major, but, hey, God hands you lemons, slice them up and stick them in your Everclear. Anyway, I'm a people person."

A mysterious rhythmic noise had been interfering more and more with the fuzzy sound of Ken's voice. Now Joyce realized that it was the sound of Sherry's dad's increasingly ragged breathing. "How dare you," he gasped. "You little fucking bastard. . . ."

"Whoa, whoa, Brother Whatever! Remember Whose presence you're speaking in. Don't you know that whenever two or more people gather in the name of God, He appears? Well, you and me are gathered in the name of Fuck, and that's all the God I'll ever need."

"You cruel little shit. What makes you think you can call me up and tell me lies about my little girl?"

"Uh. What makes you think I can't? Anyway, don't call me a liar, dude. I'm so totally on the level."

"Bullshit. Don't you ever call here again."

"Hey, hey, hey! Don't hang up yet! Look, man, I'll prove it to you. When Sherry was a little baby, you used to give her baths, right? Like in the sink or some cute shit like that?"

"Shut up. Shut your filthy trap. I'm warning you."

"Don't warn me. Now, see, if you'd said 'begging' instead of 'warning,' it might've made a difference. And also, '*please* shut your filthy trap.' Anyway, when you were being all paternal with naked baby Sherry, you must have noticed that little birthmark high up on her right inner thigh. You know the one? Just a few inches away from her labia? Well, that's how far away it is now, at least. Back then who knows. Well, I mean, you do."

Sherry's dad made a funny noise. Joyce didn't think it was a word.

"Don't get mad at me, man, I didn't put it there. Anyway, I haven't seen it, but all the guys who've fucked her have told me about it, and, believe me, that's an awful lot of guys. Like, this sort of leathery brown square patch, although one guy said it looked like a swastika, and another dude actually wanted a refund, because it looked like a smushed booger. But don't worry, we don't give refunds on your daughter's pussy. See, sir, I stick up for Sherry's honor."

Sherry's dad was wheezing and he had trouble yelling: "You . . . fucking . . . keep your *hands* off . . . ."

"Huh? Dude, I told you, I haven't fucked her yet. But, anyway, I told you I'm calling to try to get you to steer Sherry away from some bad decisions. See, she found this real pushover john who says he loves her and shit like that, *you* know how us guys are, and so now she's talking about quitting. Normally I wouldn't much give a shit, since, frankly, she's kind of a bitch. Pardon my saying so, sir, but maybe if you'd kicked her in the belly a little more when she was growing up, she wouldn't be so spoiled. But anyway, my point is that it seems sort of shitty to let her retire now, because I'm just about to introduce a dental plan for all my girls."

Sherry lost it for real right when her father did. He exploded into impotent howls and, upon hearing her father reduced that way, Sherry emitted a sound that made Joyce jump: a low, mournful, defeated groan, a pure sonic distillation of suffering. With a thrill Joyce realized this was the first real glimpse she'd ever had of someone's soul. Sherry leaped off of the couch, nails going for Ken's eyes—Joyce had no chance to yank her back, so she stuck out her leg just in time to trip Sherry and send her sprawling onto her face at Ken's feet. She landed pretty hard. Joyce glanced sheepishly at Mal, who was holding the bridge of her nose between her thumb and forefinger and shaking her head. Meanwhile, Ken expressionlessly studied Sherry's reactions as her father's rage continued to spew from the speaker, spurred on by Ken's delighted voice. Sherry, mouth against the carpet, set up a howl, but then it seemed like some invisible force cut off her windpipe. Ken said, "You got my Melissa to break up with me? I got your dad to break up with you. Tenfold, baby."

Sherry roared. "Why'd you tell my daddy?!!"

Joyce winced. She tried to say something, but her mouth was dry, and she had no clue what to say. Mal was rooting through Sherry's purse, a girly bag with a brand name stamped on the side. "What are you doing?" Joyce demanded, shouting to be heard over the commotion.

For a second it seemed like Mal would ignore the question. Then she said, "I'm hoping she has that guy Bryce's number written down in here somewhere."

"Why?"

"Somebody has to take her home. I've got to go to work, and I don't think we should ask her dad."

Ken stood with his arms crossed, looking down like a scientist on the mangled wreck of the girl at his feet. "Why my daddy?!!!" Her voice sounded like nails being scraped down a blackboard in a cave under deep water. It seemed from the redness of Sherry's face that her heart was pumping all its blood there alone, and it occurred to Joyce that there was something crazy about this fit, something beyond Sherry being just plain furious, horrified, and broken. She hoped Mal would find Bryce's number and she wouldn't have to look after Sherry herself. "Ken," she said. "That's enough."

Ken looked at her. "I'm not doing anything anymore," he mildly pointed out.

Mal sighed, checked her watch, and dumped Sherry's purse out on the floor. She sifted through the junk, oblivious to Sherry's inarticulate cry. Finally, in triumph, Mal held up a scrap of paper and went into Ken's bedroom, which was where he kept the phone. He didn't make a fuss about no one having asked him if it was okay to use his telephone, too absorbed in the ongoing experiment. Joyce watched him.

Sherry gradually wore down. Her raggedy throat couldn't scream anymore. Now there were just moans, punctuated by shallow breaths. These subsided into wheezings and whimpers. She didn't move; she lay on her belly on the stained floor, fists hiding the sides of her face.

Once it was clear that she wasn't going to holler anymore, Ken got bored. He said to Joyce, "Those guys ought to be showing up soon. You can fuck one of them or not, I don't care, tell them both to get lost if you want to. I'm going to smoke a joint in the back, so if you do stick around don't use that room. Tell Mal she can stop using the closet if she wants, since there's only two of you now. Which is how many it was supposed to be in the first place. I'll still charge her the same price."

Joyce remembered that one time up in the Honors Forum when he'd put his hands all over her tits, and she'd pretended like it was all a big joke and had admired his audacity. Now she understood how it hadn't mattered that she was his platonic friend. Or, rather, it had been necessary to make her a platonic friend so that the laying of the hands on the tits would mean something. Joyce whispered gently to Sherry and tried to coax her up off the floor. But she couldn't get any response at all.

Mal came back and said that Bryce was hurrying over to pick her up. "What a fucking dumb-ass waste," she said, and Joyce was unsure whether Mal was referring to Bryce being wasted on such melodramatic skag, or to the destruction Ken had wrought, or what. But who gave a shit.

Soon they heard Bryce's car screech to a stop before the front yard, and then he'd burst in with red eyes and went straight for Sherry. He murmured something to her that persuaded her to get up. "I don't have no daddy no more," Sherry gasped. Bryce shushed her. The two johns showed up as Bryce was taking care of Sherry, and had to be convinced that, no, no one was going to fuck them after all. They consoled themselves by smirking at the sight of Bryce leading Sherry out, her shuffling along like a stroke victim. The johns recognized Sherry—she'd fucked one of them—and they figured this spectacle was the aftermath of Bryce having discovered his girlfriend was a whore. They had a laugh over his red eyes and geekiness, and the extreme state of pussy-whippedness he must be in not to be beating the shit out of the girl. Then they took off.

With the lovers gone, Joyce walked Mal to her car. Neither of them said goodbye to Ken. Mal climbed in, turned the ignition, and made a wry face at Joyce. "And then there were three," she said.

She pulled out of the driveway. Joyce waved after her and then began the walk to campus. Mal's remark confused her until it dawned on her that Mal was including Ken.

10.

Joyce assumed the brothel was finished. She and Mal were scheduled to fuck again on Friday, which would give her plenty of time to call Ken and give notice, so he wouldn't wind up with a couple of sullen johns on his couch. She would do that—be nice, professional, grown-up. Then she'd give herself a couple weeks to cool off before hanging out with him again. This was her plan as she opened the door to her dorm room the next day, saw Mal smoking on the windowsill, flung her backpack onto the floor, and plopped onto her narrow bed. For a little while they didn't speak. Even with the window open, the air was acrid with smoke.

At last Joyce said, "I don't guess you're going over to Ken's on Friday, are you?"

"Sure. Why not?"

Joyce stared at her. "After all that shit that went down yesterday? Are you serious?"

"The only thing different is that Sherry won't be there."

"But Ken was such an asshole. I mean, Mal, he was *such* an *asshole*."

"Like I said: the only thing different is that Sherry won't be there. There was always a lot of ugliness inherent in the whole thing."

"Inherent is one thing. Screaming and blubbering in my face is another."

"Same thing to me."

"Jesus Christ, you're tough."

"It's easy money. But I can see why you wouldn't want to go back. Anyway, you don't need the extra cash."

There wasn't anything in Mal's tone that wasn't simply matter-of-fact. Nevertheless, Joyce ducked her head and concentrated on her chewed-up nails. "Naw, every little bit helps. I just figured you weren't going to show up. But if you're going, then, you know. I'm still down."

Mal gazed out the window and took another drag of her cigarette.

After Mal left for Foxy's, Joyce listened to her stereo for a while, then decided to turn in early. She was brushing her teeth when she heard the door in the next room open. Cringing at the thought of seeing Sherry, she decided to rinse her mouth as quietly as possible, turn off the light, slip under the covers, and, if Sherry knocked, make like she'd been sleeping for hours. But then she heard a low, solicitous male voice, and Sherry's unsteady reply. So Bryce was in there. The temptation to get some juicy tidbit outweighed her dread of seeing Sherry. Joyce arrested the motion of her toothbrush so as to be absolutely quiet, continuing to hold the thing in her mouth as if she were a statue. If someone entered, she would start brushing again, giving herself an excuse for being here within such easy earshot. She had a clear picture of sweet, worried Bryce escorting an invalid Sherry across the room to her bed, holding her elbow.

They spoke in tones too low to be made out clearly, but Joyce could tell that Bryce was asking if there was anything else he could do, and Sherry was replying with one-syllable grunts .... Footsteps toward the bathroom! Joyce started brushing her teeth again. From the steady tread she knew this was Bryce, walking alone and not escorting Sherry. He opened the door and recoiled when he saw Joyce. Then he grimaced and glanced sidelong at Sherry, somewhere out of Joyce's sight, and entered, pulling the door closed behind him. "Sorry," he whispered delicately, as if Sherry's condition was so precarious that she couldn't be allowed even the mild shock of learning that Joyce was in the bathroom.

Joyce tried to smile and whisper "That's okay" through a mouthful of foam. She spat and rinsed while Bryce stood there with his hands in his pockets, looking uncomfortable. Obviously he had come there to pee, but was too delicate to say so to Joyce (apparently fucking whores in a brothel had been more delicate). He couldn't leave and come back in a few minutes, because he didn't want to tell Sherry that Joyce was there and conjure up the girls' last meeting. He was at a loss.

Joyce ignored his dilemma. "How is she?" she asked, making her concerned face.

Bryce shoved his hands deeper into his pockets and raised his bony shoulders even higher, looking down at his shoes. "Pretty bad," he murmured. "I've been having to beg her to eat. And she won't call her father, even though I keep telling her it's best to get it over with as soon as possible."

"Uh. I don't know about *that*," Joyce whispered.

Bryce looked at her like she'd also suffered some trauma. "But he'll still *love* her."

"Well. I mean, not necessarily."

Bryce shook his head. "Nobody could stay mad at Sherry. Nobody would have the heart to." His fists bunched up in his pockets, and his whisper turned sandpapery. "I mean, how could that asshole do that to her? It's the meanest thing I've ever even heard of. I never thought evil people really existed, you know? I thought they were only in books and movies."

"Oh, I don't think Ken's *evil*, exactly. . . ."

"Then what the heck do you call a prank like that?! I told you, she can barely eat!"

"I'm not saying there's nothing wrong with him. Just, I kind of know where he's coming from."

Bryce's fists came out of his pockets. The volume of his voice stayed low, but it got harder. "You hate Sherry that much, huh?"

"No! I just mean, I guess I've done the same sort of thing before."

"You have? As what that guy did to Sherry?"

"Oh, kind of. My first boyfriend, when I was thirteen and he was seventeen." Joyce forced a laugh and waved her hands dismissively. "You know, he sort of blew his brains out and all that."

"What? Jeez. Why?"

"Oh, you know, because of me, sort of." Joyce wondered why she was still talking. A flat sheen had covered her field of vision, and microscopic red-hot needles were being inserted into every pore of her face.

Bryce looked all concerned and kind and sweet and stuff. "What do you think you did?"

Joyce backed out of the bathroom, laughing and forgetting to whisper. "Oh, you know, I made fun of him, and I was like Ken." She shut the bathroom door behind her and switched off the light and got into bed.

The next day Joyce vomited twice before leaving for the brothel, like an amateur. As she knelt on the tile with her head in the toilet bowl, she found herself unable to erase the image of Ken standing with his arms crossed, looking unfeelingly down upon her dying comrade.

She was late to the brothel, but so were the johns—there was no sign of them. Ken was on the floor doing homework, and Mal was smoking on the loveseat.

"Where are they?" Joyce shouted.

Ken jumped as if he were actually startled, though it was impossible to tell for sure. "Why, you on a schedule or something?"

"God damn you, Ken. You're fucking with us."

He rolled his eyes and returned to the notebook on his lap. "They're *late*, all right? Jesus. Now just sit down, for fuck's sake, and be quiet. This paper's due on Monday."

Joyce plopped down on the sofa and crossed her arms. Mal watched her smolder at Ken. In a desperately provocative way, Joyce said, "How bourgeois, Ken. Doing fucking *homework*."

Without looking up or pausing the motion of his pen, Ken

murmured, "I *am* bourgeois, duh. My mom bought my fucking car for me, for fuck's sake."

"Well, you sure seemed cutting-edge the other day. That little show you produced, with Sherry."

"There's nothing very cutting-edge about a father disowning a fornicating daughter, dude. It's the oldest trick in the patriarchy."

"Well, she's a wreck now."

"She was always a wreck. She's only a bigger wreck now because she's got that sucker there to be all concerned and clean up after her. Look, you're not going to go all boring too, are you?"

"Or what? You'll call *my* step-father and tattle on *me*?"

"Nah. I'd have to think of something else. Calling Daddy wouldn't have the same emotional impact for you, since you've never exactly been his little princess. . . . But then again, wasn't the whole point of all this shit originally to piss him off?"

Joyce blinked. "Oh yeah." She tried to stay hard, but some of the old amusement seeped in through the cracks. "At the Dixie Café. That was fun."

Ken wasn't paying attention to his homework anymore—he looked straight at Joyce, a glimmer in his eye. "Shit. I forgot about that, too. . . . So. What do you think?"

"About *telling* him?" asked Joyce, with a mix of giddy terror and delight.

"Like I said, wasn't that the point, once?"

"Sure was. . . . We couldn't do it the same way you did with Sherry."

"Of course not. Variety's, like, the spice of life."

"Exactly."

They could have kept going. But Mal ground out her cigarette and said, "Looks like the customers are here."

Through the narrow doorframe came two beefy boys, red-faced, smirking, entitled, and huge. Only now that the aloe of relief swelled inside her did Joyce realize how frightened she'd been of Ken pulling some prank on her, how nearly sure she'd been that she would look up to see Atchley. Instead, they were the two boys who'd been turned away last time, due to Sherry's freak-out. Joyce had to stop and concentrate in order to remember whether she had ever fucked either of these guys. She decided she hadn't. The big one on the left was working a plug of tobacco with his jaws, periodically spitting the stinky brown juice into a Dixie cup that he carried. That was gross, but there was a hint of nervous human goofiness about him, whereas his partner had a sneer pasted to his face that chilled Joyce's guts.

As Ken introduced them all, Joyce caught Mal's eye and gave her a surreptitious, pleading look. It had to be quick, lest it be noticed by one of the three guys, and Joyce didn't think Mal could have registered it. More, she couldn't see any reason why Mal would want to do Joyce such a big favor, especially when Joyce had never told her about the hideousness with Atchley. Yet Mal, for whatever reason, rose immediately after Joyce sent her that distress call, and selected the sneerer. Joyce tried to remain discreet for now, but told herself that afterwards she would express her gratitude to Mal. They sat through the spiked bat speech one last time, though they did not yet know that it was the last time. Then Joyce led her boy by the hand back to the marijuana room. Mal followed with her john, stopping in Ken's bedroom. Ken sat on guard in the living room, his spiked bat within easy reach.

Mal began taking off her shirt as soon as the doors were closed. While the T-shirt was still over her head, the john, who stood in the middle of the room, transfixed, fingers wiggling at the ends of his limp arms, said, "Hurry up and get your pants off, bitch."

Mal folded her shirt over the back of Ken's desk chair, then reached around to unhook her bra. "I'm already getting undressed."

"Bitch, I said your *pants*!"

"Okay, okay, don't wet yourself." Laying her bra over the shirt, Mal kicked off her shoes, then undid her zipper. "Why don't you go ahead and crawl into bed and get ready for me?"

The john shook his head like she'd tried to outsmart him. "Uh-*uh*, bitch. I'm ready *now*. And *I'm* on top. No bitch gets on top of me."

When fucking strangers—especially creepy ones—Mal preferred the relative control and safety of the top position. But they were paying customers, after all, and she supposed it was reasonable that their predilections be taken into account. Plus, it was hard for Mal to be scared of anyone. She shrugged and took off her panties, then stood before the john with her hands on her hips. "Let's see your dick," she said. He hadn't put her in a very delicate mood.

"Uh-*uh*, bitch, I'm calling the shots now. Now *get* your ass in that bed."

"For Christ's sake, it's called a visual check. It's an industry standard. They do it at the Mustang Ranch."

The john's leer faltered. He didn't know what the Mustang Ranch was.

Mal pointed at her crotch. "You see this pussy? Well, this is as close as you're going to get to it, unless you give me a look at your dick."

A sheen of sweat materialized on the john's forehead. Then his sneer made a comeback: "Go ahead," he said. "But *you've* got to whip it out."

"Sure." She stepped forward, undid his pants, and took his penis out. It was already tumescent—a bonus, since Mal had pegged him as either a guy who would finish lickety-split, or who was well-nigh impotent and would require an annoying bout of coaxing. The top of his dick seemed fine. Mal got on her knees to check its underside and his balls. The area reeked of an acrid, pungent mash of urine, sweat, and smegma. What with her face being so close to his package, the john's breathing had audibly changed. Rising to her feet, Mal picked up a condom from Ken's desk and held it out to the john. "Want me to put it on you?" she asked, suspecting he might not know how to do it.

He snatched it from her: "*Get* in that bed!" Mal wordlessly obeyed.

Lying flat and dead-like on her back, she watched as he put on the condom, to make sure he really did it. Then he climbed on top of her with all his clothes on. Mal stifled a laugh, despite being under no illusion that what was coming would be pleasant. He rammed himself inside her and grunted with pleasure or exertion. Even without foreplay things were not too painful for Mal; she was able to exercise great control over her body, and in another compartment of her mind had already concentrated on a very different and wholly imaginary scene hard enough to lubricate herself. The john doghumped her in arrhythmic bursts, while she laid her hands on him only enough to hold him roughly in place. She thought about the Astronomy class she'd had that day, and the rapid expansion of the universe; also, ways to increase her tips at Foxy's.

Abruptly the john stopped. Mal just figured he had finished so unspectacularly that she hadn't even felt it. He'd been pretty fast, too, which was nice. But then he lifted his red sweaty head and said, "Now you're going to suck my dick, bitch."

"No way," she said, hearing the plop of his dick withdrawing from her body. "I only do that for immaculately clean dicks. I mean pink and smooth and reeking of baby powder. Your dick smelled like a swamp, and that was before we got it all covered in spermicide and my own vaginal juices."

Affronted, the john said, "Bitch, who's fucking paying you?!"

"I think you have an inflated idea of how exorbitant my fee is. You give me a million dollars, plus go scrub up in the shower for a hundred years, and I'll pop it in my mouth for maybe half a second."

The john turned red and his breathing got heavy; his face literally swelled, and Mal, curious, wondered if she was going to get hit. "You *cunt*," he gasped. Somewhere on the psychological plane she had done something to him which bore only an accidental relation to her real-world actions. Then he did it! He slapped her! A little cuff across the mouth with the palm of his left hand. Because they were in such close quarters, he wasn't able to put much force behind the blow. Mal's eyes widened and she burst into laughter. "Oooo!" she exclaimed.

This enraged the john, and he slowly and laboriously reared back to get better leverage. Mal reflected that it was a lucky thing he wasn't trying to strangle her; the big lug probably would have managed that. He drew back his left hand, glaring down at her with hatred. Mal grinned and waggled her eyebrows. "Don't fuck up, now," she advised.

He backhanded her, this time getting a respectable slap in. Mal felt her teeth cut the inside of her lip, and she tasted blood. Laughing harder, she cried, "Hey, Ken! Get in here and whack this asshole for me!"

Had he been waiting just beyond the door? Ken burst in immediately, brandishing the spiked bat. He danced over to the edge of the bed, and then, after executing a twirl he had seen many times in *Conan the Barbarian*, he brought the spiked bat firmly down on the john's ass, business-end first.

The john had only been staring at Ken in amazement. Once punctured, though, he first gasped, and then let out a howl.

Mal laughed. Ken studied the pierced john. "You want me to take it out?" he asked Mal.

"You'd better," said Mal, "otherwise I'll be stuck under the big galumph forever."

The john looked back down at Mal and took a time-out from yowling and weeping to sob, *"You bitch!"*

"Tsk tsk," said Ken, and wiggled the nail around. Judging from the john's reaction, this was excruciating. "Don't make me rip you a new asshole."

"Come on," said Mal, still amused, "leave him mobile. I don't want to be suffocated."

"Well, the spike is kind of wedged into his butt."

The door to the marijuana room flew open and Joyce and her john rushed in, wrapped in blankets. "I heard—" began Joyce, and then the pair lurched to a speechless halt before the grisly tableau. "He didn't buy the speech," Ken said. "Spell must not've worked." The pierced john upped the ante, volume-wise. "Take it out!" begged Joyce's client.

"Yeah," Mal agreed, shoving against the guy's bulky

shoulders, "let's get a move on."

"Oh, well," said Ken, regretfully. He yanked the nail out, eliciting a little yelp from the john. Now Ken held the spiked bat like he was standing in the on-deck batter's box, ready to pounce. "Nice and easy now," he said. "You just hop off the nice lady now, big fellow, and no monkey business."

"You leave him alone!" cried the uninjured, tear-streaked john.

"Sure, so long as he doesn't hurt anyone," Ken said. He sounded very reasonable. Joyce's breathing had gotten rapid and shallow, and she remained speechless.

The john eased himself off of Mal, sniffling and yelping and groaning, and got shakily to his feet. Mal slid off the bed and made a beeline for her clothes; Joyce couldn't remember ever having seen Mal grin like that before. The wounded john was trying to pull up and fasten his pants with trembling hands, the blood flowing from his ass staining jeans and underwear.

Ken stood in front of him, spiked bat at the ready. "You tell anybody and we'll tell your mom," he nonchalantly said. The john sniffed.

Seeing the blood drip from the nail, Joyce felt a wave of nausea. She realized that, given the positions of the two boys and the way Ken was holding the bat, if he were to swing now he would get the john in the head. Maybe not in the temple or anything. But in the jaw, maybe. She found her voice, albeit only enough to say, "Jesus, Ken."

"You asshole," added her boy. He kept plenty far back from the rogue pimp, though.

"What?" A stranger might have bought Ken's hurt expression (Joyce's bewildered john did buy it, in fact). "I read the speech! I made sure everyone was quiet during it! So what the fuck?"

Joyce could only repeat, "Jesus," shaking her head.

Mal made a derisive noise as she slipped the T-shirt back over her head. Then she grinned at Joyce and with a jolt Joyce saw for the first time that Mal's mouth was bloody. "Fuck him,

Joyce. He was hitting me, so I called Ken to take care of the piece of shit. Don't you know that's what pimps are for?"

The uninjured john snapped at her: "Well, if you're so upset, how come you're fucking laughing now? Huh?"

Mal looked at him coolly. "I'm not laughing," she said, "I'm smiling. And I didn't say he upset me. I just said he hit me."

Joyce continued to shake her head at Ken, who said, "Well, *jeez*! I'm *sorry*!" He threw his hands up in an I-couldn't-help-it gesture, and in the process swung the bat and hit the wall with a whack loud enough to make everyone but himself and Mal jump. "He was beating on her so I whammed him."

"It's true," Mal said to Joyce. "The guy's a pig." The johns didn't protest; Joyce's was busy fussing over his buddy, who was whimpering and struggling to shut up and control himself manfully.

Joyce sighed. "Well, I guess we'll have to give them both freebies, anyway."

Mal was kneeling to tie her shoes. Now her hands froze, and she looked up and locked eyes with Joyce, all traces of a smile suddenly gone. "No," she said. "My job is to lie down and get fucked and I did that. I'll be damned if I'm going to give this loser a hundred-percent discount because he beat on me."

"Yeah," said Ken, eyeing Joyce as if she were a little nuts. "No fucking way I'm going to go without my commission the one time I actually do my job."

They ushered the sullen, shaken boys out, which wasn't too hard. Getting paid was only slightly more difficult—the doubly-assholed john made some indignant noises about it, but Ken standing there with his spiked bat proved to be an effective motivator. For her part, Joyce waived her client's debt, preferring to pay Ken's commission out of her own pocket.

Mal skipped out to her car and left as soon as she'd received her payment and given Ken his tiny cut, ignoring his protests at the lack of a bonus.

11.

Joyce still hung out with Sherry occasionally (and Bryce along with her—that guy got more boring every day); but Mal she didn't see a whole lot of, once everything had been called off. With the money Mal made stripping, she'd moved out of the dorm and gotten an apartment; she had a roommate, some tattooed chick. Sometimes Joyce thought she ought to ring old Mal up, invite her out for a pizza in the student center, just because it was a good idea to keep in touch with people. And because she was curious. Did Mal still fuck any of the old guys, herself? Did she feel elegaic, embarrassed? Relieved? They sometimes passed each other on campus, or bumped into one another in town, and they usually stopped and talked a while, Mal with that distant expression. But Joyce never properly invited her out. Maybe Mal lived in a whole different dimension—maybe that was all horseshit.... Joyce was a little scared of Mal. Was she human in the same way Joyce was? Was there a secret trauma, the singularity at her vacuum core?

Mal rarely spoke to anyone. But the work, dead as it was, naturally followed her around. There was some sniggering on campus, but she was glacial. One guy, though, gave her a lot of shit. She couldn't remember his name, but he was the one who'd manipulated his urethra as if it were a puppet's mouth. He sat with some other frat boys behind her in Astronomy, and they would spend all period nudging each other and whispering and (though they would have called it "laughing") giggling. The seating was tiered, and whenever the prof turned to face the whiteboard they would throw spitballs and folded-up notes down at her. She never changed her seat, nor read their notes. No one would sit next to her after a while.

One day, as she walked into class, she found Dick Puppet lying in wait for her just inside the doorway. He blocked her way and beamed down at her, grinning with perfectly straight, yellow teeth, as if his parents had gotten him braces but he had never bothered to use his toothbrush. "Hey, baby," he said. "Remember me?"

"Yes," she said. "You were memorably forgettable."

"What's that supposed to mean?"

"See?"

He kept up his dopey grin. "I got some friends want to meet you."

"You mean those boys with the dicks bigger than yours?"

His grin faded momentarily, but then he recovered, saying, "You ain't seen their dicks."

"Sure I have. They're sticking up out of their shirts."

He laughed—*haw! haw!*—like he thought they were making witty conversation at some sophisticated cocktail square-dance. She shouldn't have made a joke, she knew. Technically, having done so meant that they were bantering now. "Come on, baby, let me introduce you. You ought to give us a two-for-one deal."

"Oh, please. You're going to haggle with me?"

"Come on, baby, everybody likes money, don't they? Why you want to work at McDonald's or some shit when you got that beautiful pussy right there?"

"You got a little piece of tobacco on your front tooth." While he was going *haw! haw!* she pushed past him. She hadn't sounded anything but tired.

Whether he really expected to fuck her again or not, he didn't leave her alone. Whenever their paths crossed—on campus, in the grocery store, in the movie theater—he would hoot and whisper things to the guys he was with, and giggle. Then, one day, he did it when they were alone together.

She was walking to her car, which she'd parked in a secluded little parking lot a block from Ken's apartment. When she rounded the corner of the overgrown fence and stepped through the gate, she saw none other than Dick Puppet, just getting out of his truck. It wasn't a set-up—his astonished gaping was too genuine. He quickly switched to a leer. "Hey, baby," he said. "What a coincidence. Must be in the fucking stars, huh?"

She looked him up and down, then checked for bystanders. She turned back to him just as he was saying, "Hey, baby. You want to skip class, baby?"

She continued to stare evenly at him, thoughtfully chewing the bubble gum she was using to quit smoking. After she'd considered for a moment, she said, "How much money you got?"

The question stumped him for a second. Then he said, "Uh, like, fifty bucks."

"You want a blow job?"

He tried to read her expression, but no one could have done that. "You serious?"

"You got fifty bucks and a dick?"

He switched tactics: "Fifty bucks for a *blow* job?"

"Jesus. What do you care? It's your momma's money, ain't it?"

"Well. Okay, shit. Where at? Just back at that same old apartment?"

"No. I don't do anything with those people anymore. Right here's fine."

He was flabbergasted. "In the parking lot? Out*side*?"

"You dumb-ass. In my car, I mean."

Dick Puppet was watching her face closely, like he thought something was fishy. "How about my truck?"

"Uh-uh," she said, shaking her head. "I don't know what kind of shit you've got in there, and I don't trust people who throw spitballs. Plus your truck's right out in the open in the middle of the parking lot. We get arrested for public lewdness, your momma going to bail me out, too? My car's parked right up facing the wall." When he still looked hesitant, she added, "Either we do it in my car, or you can go back to playing games with your boyfriends in Astronomy."

The "boyfriends" thing got him. "All right, all right," he said. "Your car, whatever."

She nodded curtly and walked to her car, pulling her key ring out of her jeans pocket. He followed, silent at last, and went to stand uncertainly on the passenger side, waiting impatiently with his hand on the door handle while she unlocked her side, tossed her backpack in the backseat, got in, shut and locked her own door, and reached over to unlock his. He got in and sat down, slamming the door, acting like he was supposed to be there. Mal looked at him. She swallowed her gum. It had lost its flavor, anyway. He looked at her, grinned, and put his hand on her inner thigh. She didn't tell him that she'd only agreed to a blow job and to fucking move his hand. She turned in her seat to face him, and, still with that eerily blank face (which was what made him desire and hate her so much), she put her hands on his shoulders, and pulled him toward her. He tried to dive for her mouth, but she ducked her head out of the way and his face ended up between her right shoulder and her neck. "Unzip my pants," she said, "while I get a condom out of the glove box."

He licked her neck, a big sloppy swipe, and whined, "Why I got to unzip your pants for a *blow* job?"

"Because I want you to." She stretched out her left arm and opened the glove box, and began fishing around inside.

"Well, if we're doing what *you* want, how come *I* got to pay?" Nevertheless, he crammed his hand down into her crotch and started fumbling about. "Shit," he muttered, "your pants're too fucking *tight!*" His voice was too loud, so close to her ear. For no reason, he bit her on the neck hard enough to draw blood, and Mal gasped in pain and decided he would pay for that. She took the gun out of the glove box and pointed the barrel down at his dick. "Hey," she said in a normal speaking voice. "Look at this."

Feeling the gun barrel press through the denim against the head of his erect penis, he withdrew his face from her spitty, bloody neck, looked down, and yelped. He jumped up a little, but she ground the gun down harder into his crotch to hold him still. He stared down at it, breathing dangerously fast. "Hey," she said, and when he still didn't look up at her she cocked the gun and said, "Hey, asswipe. Look at me!" He did. It was amazing, the change in his face. His lips had parted, he'd gone pale, he was starting to sweat, the sound of his breathing filled the car. "Be quiet," she said, her voice still low but full of command. "Breathe quieter or I'll shoot your dick off." He didn't exactly comply, but he was obviously trying to. Mal had never seen anyone so scared, not even Sherry.

He licked his dry lips with the tip of his dry, trembling tongue. "Come on," he said, "give me a break. I was just fooling."

She leaned back against her door, considering her captured specimen. "I want you to know," she said, "I don't give a shit if you respect me, and I don't mind if you and your boyfriends keep throwing spitballs at me in class. I just wanted to tell you, just once, so you'd know, how stupid you looked, that one time, when you were pretending your dick had a mouth."

He stared at her, concentrating, the way a person terrified of flying will stare at the wing of a plane all the way across the ocean. Doubtless he would later think of all sorts of things to say to her, but by then she would be gone.

Mal tried to form her words as carefully as possible, to say exactly the right thing. "I just wanted you to know," she said, "that I'm more dangerous than you."

Now she brought the gun up, tracing it languorously up from his dick to his belly button, sternum, throat, chin. "Open your mouth," she ordered him mildly. When he hesitated, she pressed the barrel against his chin and hardened her voice: "*Open it!*" Now he obeyed, and she slipped it in, pushing the muzzle so far back in his throat that he gagged and retched and pleaded with her with his eyes. She sat up straighter, arching her back, and brought her face very close to his, feeling sexy again. "From now on," she purred, "every time, every time you get a hard-on, I want you to think about this, my gun in your mouth, my gun on your cock, and see if you can stay hard." Then, suddenly, she sat back again, pulling the gun out and banging it carelessly against his teeth. She kept it trained on him. "Get the fuck out of my car," she said, sounding bored now.

He obeyed quickly, if clumsily. Once he got the door open he fell out backwards and scooted frantically away on his ass, then froze after five feet, staring up at her in terror.

Mal had been about to drive off; but now it occurred to her that she might've fucked up. She studied this wilted boy on the other side of her gun, and watched the dark stain spreading out from the crotch of his pants. Maybe she'd pushed him too far. Maybe he'd gone past the breaking point, and maybe tomorrow, or the next day, he'd gun her down in Astronomy. It was possible. Guys who'd been jilted far more gently did the same thing all the time. Looking at him now, it occurred to her that the safest thing to do might be to kill him.

But oh well. You can't always be safe. And what was she supposed to do, shoot him right here in cold blood? She figured that would be even riskier in the long run than letting him go. The logistics would be too difficult. So she reached over, slammed and locked the passenger's door, started her engine, and drove off. And, as it turned out, he didn't kill her at all. Instead he just dropped out of Astronomy, and, when they happened to bump into each other in town, he acted like he didn't see her, and turned and walked the other way.

If you enjoyed this book, please help spread the word about it; take a moment to leave a review on Goodreads, Amazon, or any other online forum.

And please sign up for our mailing list, at saltimbanque-books.com

ACKNOWLEDGMENTS

Thank you to my editor Brian Hurley, who cut about a third of the book and then let me put some back. Much gratitude to my parents—thank you to my brother, Chris, for a lot of loans, a couple of which I repaid. Early readers included Jon Rachmani and Jacob Cockcroft. Tiffany Esteb didn't read it but she did once tell me to leave the warts in. Thank-yous to Mike Lindgren and Ron Kolm for, like, keeping the faith, or whatever. Carl Anderson agreed to read it and give me feedback but then I think I just never sent him a copy. Thank you, Emileena Pedigo. Most of the first draft was written in Australia's Gold Coast when I stayed with Rachael Walker in her family's apartment, so thank you, Rachael. There are others who should be thanked.

ALSO FROM SALTIMBANQUE BOOKS:

BENJAMIN GOLDEN DEVILHORNS, by Doug Shields

A collection of stories set in a bizarre, almost believable universe: the lord of cockroaches breathes the same air as a genius teenage girl with a thing for criminals, a ruthless meat tycoon who hasn't figured out that secret gay affairs are best conducted out of town, and a telepathic bowling ball. Yes, the bowling ball breathes.

RICKY, by J. Boyett

Ricky's hoping to begin a new life upon his release from prison; but on his second day out, someone murders his sister. Determined to find her killer, but with no idea how to go about it, Ricky follows a dangerous path, led by clues that may only be in his mind.

STEWART AND JEAN, by J. Boyett

A blind date between Stewart and Jean explodes into a confrontation from the past when Jean realizes that theirs is not a random meeting at all, but that Stewart is the brother of the man who once tried to rape her. Or is she the woman who murdered his brother? And will anyone ever know?

THE LITTLE MERMAID: A HORROR STORY, by J. Boyett

Brenna has an idyllic life with her heroic, dashing, lifeguard boyfriend Mark. She knows it's only natural that other girls should have crushes on the guy. But there's something different about the young girl he's rescued, who seemed to appear in the sea out of nowhere—a young girl with strange powers, and who will stop at nothing to have Mark for herself.

THE VICTIM *(AND OTHER SHORT PLAYS)*, by J. Boyett

In The Victim, April wants Grace to help her prosecute the guys who raped them years before. The only problem is, Grace doesn't remember things that way.... Also included:

A young man picks up a strange woman in a bar, only to realize she's no stranger after all;

An uptight socialite learns some outrageous truths about her family;

A sister stumbles upon her brother's bizarre sexual rite;

A first date ends in grotesque revelations;

A love potion proves all too effective;

A lesbian wedding is complicated when it turns out one bride's brother used to date the other bride.

COMING IN 2016:

COLD PLATE SPECIAL, by Rob Widdicombe

Jarvis Henders has finally hit the beige bottom of his beige life, his law-school dreams in shambles, and every bar singing to him to end his latest streak of sobriety. Instead of falling back off the wagon, he decides to go take his life back from the child molester who stole it. But his journey through the looking glass turns into an adventure where he's too busy trying to guess what will come at him next, to dwell on the ghosts of his past.

I'M YOUR MAN, by F. Sykes

It's New York in the 1990's, and every week for years Fred has cruised Port Authority for hustlers, living a double life, dreaming of the one perfect boy that he can really love. When he meets Adam, he wonders if he's found that perfect boy after all ... and even though Adam proves to be very imperfect, and very real, Fred's dream is strengthened to the point that he finds it difficult to awake.

THE UNKILLABLES, by J. Boyett

Gash-Eye already thought life was hard, as the Neanderthal slave to a band of Cro-Magnons. Then zombies attacked, wiping out nearly everyone she knows and separating her from the Jaw, her half-breed son. Now she fights to keep the last remnants of her former captors alive. Meanwhile, the Jaw and his father try to survive as they maneuver the zombie-infested landscape alongside time-travelers from thirty thousand years in the future.... Destined to become a classic in the literature of Zombies vs. Cavemen.

ABOUT THE AUTHOR

J. Boyett can be reached at jboyettjboyett@gmail.com, unless you are reading this many years after we went to print and no one uses Gmail anymore, and/or unless J. Boyett has died.

Made in the USA
Columbia, SC
21 November 2021

49004715R00079